Functionally Immortal

Lakeside Murders

Aleksandra Otto

To my humans who made this possible.

I don't know if I could have ever written this weird little book without any of you.

Content Warnings

On Page:
Descriptions of dead bodies
Autopsy
Depiction of knives, guns, and other weaponry
Depiction of dead animals
Depiction of open wounds
Violence
Blood
Soft drug use
Consensual sex between adults
Tentacles
Ghosts/Spirits/Undead
Supernatural Creatures
Mild Homophobia/Bi-phobia

Discussed:
PTSD
Mass Genocide
Murder
Nazi's

War
Loss of partners
Previous Injury
Hospitalization of parent

Table of Contents

Chapter 1

Tailen

The knock at my door was not unexpected. Swinging the dark wooden door of my cabin open, I was greeted with about as pleasant of a sight as a member of law enforcement can be. Summer of 1996 just got interesting.

"Miss Galloway, my name is Agent Lewis FBI, I have some questions for you." His voice was steady, if not a little stodgy. A little too much for my taste, but I could appreciate the frankness.

"I've been expecting your visit agent. Please, come in. I've put on some coffee." Stepping back from the door, I let it swing further open. His eyebrow cocked over his aviator sunglasses and he sighed, seeming a bit defeated by the invitation. I wonder if he was expecting a less welcoming person.

"The Sheriff called you? I told him not to do that.." he mumbled something about protocol as he stepped into the cabin taking off his sunglasses.

"No, it was Rose. Nothing really gets past her, so I figured you would be here about the murders. Considering the Sheriff has me pegged as his number one suspect." Shutting the door, I move to the kitchen counter. Now that he's fully inside I can finally get a better look at him.

Agent Lewis is tallish, about an inch or so taller than myself. Dusty brown hair that was parted rather haphazardly to the side, with just a hint of grey coming in over the tops of his ears. Didn't look young enough to have grey hair yet, but if he was in the Bureau, the stress may be enough. He had a little bit of dark scruff coming in fairly thick on his chin and cheeks. The line of his jaw was strong, but soft. His black suit definitely looked like he had been driving in it all day, the tie wasn't quite straight. He seemed tired. Good thing I had coffee.

"Not that you should take a drink from a murder suspect, but if you would like some." I pulled a mug from a higher shelf and turned to him, gesturing with the mug. The look on his face when I turned to him was, for lack of a better description, amusing. He stifled a cough, and looked towards the opposite wall, his face flushed. I looked down at myself to see what I had done.

I was wearing what Rose would call, "casual summer clothing". It was a cropped t-shirt with a logo from a band Rose liked on it, and a pair of denim shorts. I didn't think it was anything to be flushed about. Maybe I should put on something to cover myself, though maybe I could use his fluster to my advantage.

"I assume you wouldn't try to kill me in the first five minutes of meeting me." He attempted to right himself and straightened his tie. "I'll take the coffee Miss Galloway, cream and sugar." He looked around the cabin. "The way Sheriff Southland described you, I would have expected.....well not this."

My cabin was small, basically one large room with a small bathroom off to the back past the sleeping area, set up on stilts from the ground. Underneath was a workshop, and where I kept my three wheeled trike and extra supplies. The main room was dark, the curtains on the two windows were pulled back letting in a small amount of light. Dust could be seen swirling in the rays that settled down on the wooden floors of the old building. The kitchen area was to the front, towards the door. It had a small round table and chairs that came from a local thrift store made of pine painted red. The cabinets matched the wood of the floor and walls, but I had taken the doors off them and painted the insides white. That made the mismatched dishes easier to see in the dimly lit room. There was a queen sized bed situated further down one wall. That admittedly hadn't been made for weeks, with a low table next to it. A dresser stood near the door to the bathroom, faded paint on it matching the look of the rest of my furniture. A small sofa pushed up against the foot of the bed, it was leather and probably the nicest quality of any of the furniture I had chosen for my home. One of those large cabinet style wooden televisions sat gathering dust across from it. It mainly served as a shelf for books and tchotchkes. The wooden walls of the cabin were lined with shelves of all sorts, covered in books, bottles, plants, and all manner of items I had picked up from the world. It would seem cluttered to some, but for me, it was perfect. I suspected however he was not speaking about the room we were standing in.

"I'm not what you expected? Did he not show you my mug shot?" I shook my head a little as I poured the hot coffee into the blue ceramic mug. Though subtle, he made a bit of a face to my statement. I gestured to the chair at the table and slid the coffee towards him, made mostly to his liking.

Sitting down across the table I leaned back in my chair, crossing my legs with a foot underneath me.

"I did get your file from him, but I only glanced at it before heading over here. I was hoping you could clear up why the Sheriff suspects you of murder Miss Galloway." His tone was very, back to business. He already found a way to avoid questions that made him slightly uncomfortable. Not that his face gave away much, save when it flushed. Even then he seemed to be trying to hide his expression.

"Call Me Tailen. I'm not used to being addressed so formally, I find it odd. As for the Sheriff, you may want to take a look at why I have the mug shot."

The folder that had been tucked under his arm was now sitting on the table open, my mug shot clearly visible on the page. Such a bad photograph. Even though it captured my choppy black hair, espresso colored eyes, and pale skin well, the little bit of my tattoos you could see, left something to be desired. They ended up having to use an old 35mm camera to take my picture and it was really rather blurry. For some reason they couldn't get a clear picture on their newer digital one. Technology wasn't always the answer in my opinion. His eyes scanned the page, those thick dark eyebrows of his didn't give much away in expression.

"You threw his son through a window."

"I did in fact, but as you can see. Charges dropped."

"Why, Miss Galloway, did you throw his son through a window?" He pinched the bridge of his nose, seeming annoyed that he had to ask the question.

"I'm not sure how that is relevant to why I'm not a murderer but to put a point on it, he deserved it. He was harassing a 17 year old girl in the hardware store."

"So you threw him through the front window? You do know that you are not helping yourself here." He sipped his coffee and looked down at the cup after the sip, making an approving mouth gesture before sipping again.

"I'm fully aware that the Sheriff has bias against me because I'm not from here, and I didn't allow his adult son to harass a young girl. I won't apologize for that. It doesn't mean that I killed four people, Agent Lewis." I could feel the serious look on my face form, pushing my brows together and wrinkling my nose.

"He claims you were at the first two crime scenes before he banned you from coming anywhere near them. Said you looked almost amused at the scene."

"He would say that wouldn't he?" I clicked my tongue and cracked my neck to one side looking at the ceiling. " I wasn't the only person when they found the bodies, crime like that happens everyone in town shows up. Plus *Bear Rest Hollow* is starting its tourist season, so there are even more people. Which is why I'm sure our lovely police force is trying to tie this up in a neat little bow as fast as possible."

"I haven't looked over the files yet, but is there any physical evidence they have that you were involved in anyway?" His fingers trailed over the pages, flipping through the few detailing the arrest, and general complaints the Sheriff had about me.

"I wouldn't imagine so, Agent. Considering I didn't kill any of them. Only thing I have killed in the last few weeks was a bear."

Now I finally see more of an expression on the Agent's face. He didn't believe me, which was the first time in this conversation he seemed to not.

"A bear? You hunt?" His voice carried disbelief through the northern Californian accent.

"Sal, the mechanic in town, is a friend of mine. He's got a contract with the mayor to make sure that any nuisance animals are taken care of. The bear had gotten a hold of a hiker ...did a number on him. We took care of it."

"The police failed to mention that you may be armed." Again muttering something as he sipped his coffee about disclosure protocols, and jotting down Sal's name. "I think the officer at the desk mentioned to me he found one of the bodies."

"I don't have any firearms, don't worry. I have the skin on a rack down in the workshop if you want to see it, and yeah he did. I'm sure you will be out to talk with him soon." I lean back in the chair lifting my arms over my head to stretch. I feel my shirt lifting slightly as I do so, the fabric stopping just below my breasts. Exposing my stomach, large sigil tattoo, and the scar covering most of my side. A deep sigh escaped my lips, these murders had put a damper on the start of summer.

Hearing a grunt from his side of the table and the papers shuffling, I came back down from my stretch to the sight of his red ears and flushed face.

"I think that we are done here for today. I'm not sure if the Sheriff was quite honest with me in his suspect pool." He closed the folder quickly and kept his eyes averted away from me, looking at one of my many shelves as a way to distract himself.

"You know agent, if I wasn't in your suspect pool, I think you wouldn't be trying to avoid looking at me. Your face keeps turning the same shade as my table." I smiled and placed my feet on the ground, I leaned forward on the table into one of my hands. It was at this moment that I understood what was making him uncomfortable. It wasn't the prospect of interviewing a suspect, I was distracting to him. Or maybe it had just been a while and I wasn't wearing enough clothing.

"I'm not sure what you mean Miss Galloway. " his face went serious as did his tone. Damn.

"Ah, never mind then. However, as an apology let me give you the name of someone who the Sheriff probably left off the suspect list." I held out my hand and gestured for the pen he held in the breast pocket of his white dress shirt. I made sure to let a finger graze his hand as i took the pen from him.

"I will look into them, I'm sure other folks around town will want to add to the list as well. Small town gossip and all."

"I'm sure if anyone else wants to, Rose will. She runs the café on main, across from the police station." I handed him the pen back after jotting on the outside of my folder the name Harold Hanson, as I did it seemed to click in his mind how she was the one to call me.

"I'll be sure to pay her a visit." Agent Lewis' tone was annoyed. He stood and made his way to the door. "Thank you for the coffee Miss Galloway."

As he headed down the steps from the front door I leaned on the door frame, watching him walk back to his large black SUV. The agent's legs were thick, and I could just make out the shape of his backside in his dress pants. He paused for a brief moment to check the pager at his hip. I yelled after him.

"It's Tailen. I'll see you soon, agent. Tell Rose I said hi."

I watched as he pulled away on the road back towards town shifting my weight back on the door before going in and closing it.

This Summer just got more interesting.

Chapter 2

Mikhail

The sigh of aggravation I let out as soon as my car door was closed was so loud I'm surprised Miss Galloway didn't hear it from her door.

Ran my fingers through my hair, and then the back of my head ruffling the short locks, hoping to rub away some of the irritation before starting up the SUV. I turned over the engine and pulled out onto the state route headed back to town. I would deal with the Sheriff and his dramatics later.

The man had made such a huge deal about me going to investigate Miss Galloway before I did anything else. He spoke about her as if she was some sort of hardened criminal. Saying she was a danger to the town, and had been nothing but a problem since she moved into that old run-down place outside of town. I should have looked at the file better before I drove all the way out there. What a blowhard. I should know better than to take the word of a man who drinks coffee that smells that burnt.

I had been expecting a woman who would be combative or at least uncooperative. Miss Galloway was everything but that. My mind floated to her reaching for the coffee mug, those denim shorts riding up, exposing the curve of her cheeks. Her speaking softly in an accent I couldn't quite place. I could feel my face turning red again. You would think at 38 years old a pair of legs wouldn't get up under my skin. That when she leaned back in the chair, thinking I would love to see how the rest of her stomach tattoo looked.

"Christ Mikhail, keep your mind on work." I said to myself out loud, hitting the steering wheel of the car with my palm to help myself focus on driving and getting back into town. The drive to her cabin had taken me about 15 minutes outside of the main drag of town, and it was just now I could see some of the roadside signs for tourism starting to dot the sides of the road.

Bear Rest Hallow: if there was a name for a tourist trap town that would be it. The town was old, and found new life in the last decade as a vacationing spot for those seeking 'outdoor' adventure. Meaning city people pay good money to stay in cabins, kayak, and have locals take them fishing. The buildings were worn, but clean. As I drove towards the center of town, it was as one would expect for a small midwestern town. Buildings butted up against each other, a strip of cars parked along the streets.

The center of town held the courthouse and the police station, as well as some green space with some rather impressive looking old trees. It seemed well tended to, though most of the gardens did, as I drove though. Tourism board knew what they were doing at least. The strips of buildings around the town center were mostly small restaurants, outdoor gear shops, and offices where people could rent cabins, hire wilderness guides, or buy cheap souvenirs to take home.

One of the restaurants that stood out among the bunch was right across from the police station, and where I pulled up and parked. It was painted bright bubblegum pink, and had the name painted in big letters across the front windows: *Rose's Cafe,* even the lettering was shades of pink. Scoffed at the color as I got out of the car, it stood out for sure, but that much pink in this town? Geeze. Who in their right mind would choose that.

As I pushed the door to the cafe open, I got my answer very quickly. The place was weirdly busy for the time of day, and looked as if I had stepped back into a show from the 60's. Pristine pastel colored walls, and booths to match, and the advertisements that were hung for decoration had to have been authentic. However, it was the woman pouring coffee at the counter who was the real reason everyone was here.

This had to be Rose, Miss Galloway's acquaintance. Who gave her the heads up of my being in town. The woman has to be about a head and a half taller than myself, possibly due to the heels I could hear clicking behind the counter as she served coffee. She was the picture of perfection. In an almost eerie way, the opposite of Miss Galloway. Rose was bright blonde, hair long and pulled back with a black headband. A rose flower tucked to one side of the band. Her face was just sun kissed, no eyebrow hair or long fluttering lash out of place. Her lips were bright red, and it matched the era appropriate red and white diner uniform she wore, though she left the button at the top completely undone; I'm not sure it could have held her breasts in even if it tried. I couldn't quite put my finger on how old she looked, which was unsettling.

I made my way to the counter, and she was there pouring coffee before I even sat down on the stool. A smile spread across her face.

"Well good afternoon Sugar, I didn't expect to see you so soon. Need cream for your coffee?" The woman's voice had that accent I would expect from this area of Michigan. I nodded to the offer.

"How did you know I would be paying your friend a visit, just by seeing my car pull in front of the station?" I was doing my best to keep my tone unannoyed, though I wasn't sure it was working. I was starting to get tired, the drive and the stress of the day so far starting to hit me as I mixed the cream and sugar into the white and pink mug in front of me.

"Well, that ass hat we call a Sheriff has been in here for the last couple weeks, sitting right over there mind you," She gestured with the coffee pot towards a booth in the corner, " about how he thought she murdered those poor people, and how he would prove it, she wasn't going to get away with it, blah blah blah. Glad I didn't vote for him." Her hand gestures were the icing on the cake, mocking the sheriff while using her hand as a puppet.

I couldn't help but let out a little bit of a stifled laugh as she called him an ass hat. Which she seemed pleased with. She set the coffee pot down and placed one hand down on the counter, leaning on it slightly. I took a sip of the coffee, it tasted just like the same as I had at Miss Galloway's.

"Now Sugar, you gotta tell me, do you think my friend could be a murderer? She hasn't done anything but just survive like the rest of us in this town. Not her fault she isn't from here."

"To be honest, Miss..."

"You can call me Rose, I don't do that last name stuff. Like Cher. Suits me better."

"Alright Rose, to be honest in my line of work, anyone can kill. I have arrested people you wouldn't believe had it in them."

"Ooo, ya think I could be the murderer then Agent?" Rose leaned forward, a little giggle in her voice, that shook her ample chest. I turned my head to look over at the jukebox that seemed to be changing over its record. What was it with the women in this town so far? First Miss Galloway and that cropped shirt almost exposing her nipples, and now a giggling blonde leaning over the counter. If every woman I came across during this case was like them, I may not make it back to Detroit.

I could see why this place was so busy on an afternoon in the middle of the week. I cleared my throat and took another long sip of my coffee in an attempt to compose myself.

"I doubt you are, you have far too much work here to be out killing innocent people." She seemed satisfied with the answer, but unsatisfied with my concentration being on my coffee.

"Suppose you are right Sugar, even with the other girls, this place is busy enough I hardly have time to finish my baking everyday before the door opens in the morning." She leaned back, crossing her arms.

I yawned and shook my head a little bit.

"I will ask you however Rose, this seems to be a pretty busy spot. Have you heard anything that might be helpful for tracking down who actually did kill those four men? Miss

Galloway mentioned you may have some names to add to the suspect list."

"I haven't, but I can certainly let you know. Oooo I feel like a detective now Sugar, you know how to make a lady's day." Rose smiled brightly, and then as she was struck by a thought, she grabbed a bag from the back counter and turned back to me. "I knew you would be by, so I packed you a couple of my donuts from this morning before they were gone."

" How did..."

" Everyone stops in Sugar." She winked at me.

I just looked down at the bag, not ungrateful for the gesture. Though I have concluded that Rose was not someone I would want to get on the bad side of. I stood from the stool and plunked down some cash, along with a card that had my name and pager number on it. She waved as I took my leave from the café and headed back out into the street.

From the front of the café, I could see the center square of town, and all the businesses, along with a rather substantial library. There were more people in the street now, I guessed it was tourists arriving for a long weekend. I checked the watch on my wrist; time to head to the motel, and get myself set up.

As much as I liked my job, digging into case files wasn't my favorite part of it. I was more of a boots on the ground sort of person.

I found my motel on the far side of the town, just about two miles from the town center. Which I was glad for. I need to remember to get a map of the area, that's not just my road atlas tomorrow. It didn't have a ton of cars parked in the lot, which would change over the course of the evening I'm sure. However for now, I was grateful for the quiet.

Appropriately named *Sleeping Bear Lodge*, the neon sign out in front of the single floor motel was glowing a bright blue. The vacancy part of the sign had clearly not worked for a long time, as the tubes were partially smashed. Must be a rule that motel signs always had to have at least some sort of malfunction.

The woman at the desk was older, pleasant, and once she found out my first name decided to tell me all about her old Russian neighbor back in Toledo with the same name. I was very grateful when she finally handed me the key, didn't try to flirt with me, and sent me on my way. It's the little things apparently.

My room was around the backside of the building, which meant I could park my car directly in front of my room, so it wouldn't be much trouble to unload my vehicle. Not that I had brought much. I like to travel fairly light when not far from home. The whole trek up here only took around three hours, but after dealing with the sheriff earlier, I was ready to not listen to another human for the rest of the night.

The door of the room stuck and I had to push it open with my shoulder, having decided that one trip from the car was all I needed. I tossed the box of case files and my grey duffle onto the table that was in front of the door, and laid the hangers of extra shirts over the back of one of the chairs. Finding the light switch next to the door, I flicked on the rather yellow overhead light of the room, deciding immediately that once I found all the lamps in the room, I would not be turning that on again.

The room was, like the rest of the town, dated but clean. The slight hint of bleach in the air was at least comforting. In front of the door was a small table, and sort of kitchenette set up with a coffee pot and miniature refrigerator. The appliance was an off-white color, seemingly due to age, but at least the compressor on it was quiet enough I would be able to ignore it for sleeping. The walls were painted a tan color, with the wall over the bed at one end being wallpapered in a very 1970's orange and brown striped print. The bedding on the full sized bed matched the wall, as well as the curtains, and rug that was under the little table. I popped my head into the small bathroom. Surprisingly it was just a glass enclosed shower and not a tub. I really wasn't mad at that. Though clean, the bathroom also suffered from the sort of off-white staining that spoke to the age of the motel.

I didn't bother putting clothing away in the dresser and just tossed my jacket on the bed before loosening my tie and opening the box of case files. At least I had those donuts Rose had given me, to help stave off the pain of reading what I expect to be poorly documented crime scene notes.

"Let's see what's actually going on in this town."

I could really use another coffee.

Chapter 3

Tailen

It's been a couple days since I had my meeting with Agent Lewis. He must be keeping busy doing actual police work instead of chasing dramatized leads from our sheriff. I had spent my time finishing up the bear skin, I needed to get it to Sal. I promised him this one so his fiancée could make herself something for their new home. Before heading out for the day, I would need to shower and probably put something other than a large shirt on before heading into town.

I had my own suspicions about the murders that had been taking place over the last few weeks here in our little town. However, since the Sheriff started his accusations, I couldn't even get close enough to any of the crime scenes or talk to anyone involved, lest I give him any fuel for his nasty rumors. I'm mostly fine with people not liking me, I've lived enough places that I'm used to that sort of thing. Locals not jiving with a new member of the community is pretty normal. I'm not fine with people fearing me for no reason other than the words of a man who shouldn't have won his last election. So I have been keeping my distance, gathering what I can from visiting *Rose's cafe* and listening to the rumors, as well as visiting the library to hit the archives. Which would be a strange place to look into modern happenings a month ago, but I'm not completely sure that the killings are being done by someone living.

The first dead body showed up about three weeks ago, out by the lake. It was a man no one really knew, and had only been seen in town in passing, getting some supplies to go out camping. This actually didn't throw up any red flags for the local police, as it wasn't uncommon to find a tourist or two dead in the woods every summer. Usually messed with a bear, or drowned while drunk and jumping off a boat into the lake. I remember visiting the scene, as I had been riding my bike out that way. Just like any time something happens in the small town, there was a small group of townies hanging out behind the police tape. I recall feeling something a bit off about it. They were calling it a drowning, but the man clearly had not. He wasn't bloated, for supposedly being in the water for several days. I watched as they loaded the man into the back of an ambulance, and out of the corner of my eye noticed something on his bare arm. It looked like a serious chemical burn.

It was when the next body was found that the Sheriff started his accusations, because the man was on the road out towards my home. Rose had called me to tell me the police were headed out my way; the scene was a mile from my house. Just me showing up was enough for the Sheriff to start in on me. We argued about why I was there, he didn't like that I pointed out he had better start accusing the other 20 people who had decided to stop along the road to look at the grizzly scene. The man had been found with his chest sliced open, his internal organs had started to form a pile on his lap, and again I could see he had serious chemical burns on his skin, this time it seemed to surround the gaping wound on his torso. Sheriff tried to take me into the station that day, but luckily a deputy stepped in to pull him away before I did something regrettable.

Since then I've kept my distance from the crime scenes. Two more deaths happened, and not a lot of leads. The last of the murdered men was found at Sal's garage, and it was particularly devastating because unlike the other three who had been out of towners, he was someone we all knew. A guy named Frank Darling, he actually lived above Sal's business and worked for him some. I hadn't visited Sal since Frank's death, and now that the FBI was in town and Agent Lewis theoretically got the Sheriff off my back, I could go and see him.

I got myself dressed in a pair of black denim shorts that hugged my thighs above the knee, a thin grey shirt with some band Rose liked on it, and boots, and grabbed my crossbody leather satchel from the top of my television. Looking in the mirror before I headed out had been a good choice. My hair was sticking up in a very unflattering manner. I wet my hair thoroughly with my hands in the kitchen sink, slicking it backwards so it would dry as I took my trike in towards town. I had the bear pelt to deliver to Sal, and besides passing on my condolences for his friend, I hoped he would be able to help confirm some of my suspicions about the killings.

The old three wheel tricycle I rode around came with the cabin when I bought it. I had restored it a bit, replacing the old worn banana seat, and the worn out spoked wheels, painting the cross bars with a purple spray paint. It made getting to town fun, as well as the basket between the back wheels was great for hauling things with me. Today I had the bear pelt, wrapped in a white sheet, shoved in there. It didn't quite fit, but good enough for a couple mile ride to the garage in town. I enjoyed my rides, it let me breath fresh air, and enjoy the nature that this valley was known for. As I passed by the scene of the second murder, I got a cold feeling from the sight of it. The yellow tape still wrapped around some trees, and blood still stained the ground around the tree the man had been leaning against. Even the rain hadn't been able to wash away everything yet.

I got to Sal's a bit after lunchtime. I could hear the sound of his radio playing from about half a block away. He had always been a little hard of hearing, though as I pulled up I'm pretty sure it was more to cover the mixed sounds of him mumbling and cursing.

Sal's Garage and Towing was the only mechanic in town. He worked on everything from Mustangs to generators. He was always pretty busy, but only had a few helpers he trusted to come in and work for him a few times a week. Today, he was alone and up under the hood of a green sedan. I could hear the growl under his breath as he dropped what sounded like a wrench down into the engine block, and the clatter as it hit the concrete underneath.

"Mother Fucking...piece of..." His voice was grumbly, and low. He pulled out from under the hood and shook his head in an irritated way, muttering. It didn't take him long before his nose crinkled and he turned his head towards me. His expression softened quite a bit and he rubbed his hands down the front of his pants. "I didn't hear you ride up Tailen. How are you?"

"Considering I've been accused of murder and questioned by the FBI this week, I'm not doing as bad as I could be." I threw my leg over the seat of the trike, hopping off and embracing my approaching friend. His arms always held on so tightly when he hugged.

Sal came to town not too long after I did. For lack of a better explanation, Rose and I helped him get settled in, and we have been good friends ever since. He was a shorter fellow, with deeply tanned skin, and black hair. He didn't have much to speak of on top of his head, but grew a pretty fantastic curled mustache. However, it was currently drooped down around the corners of his mouth, from his face being sweaty due to the rising summer heat. He was a pretty furry guy, and was currently just wearing a green mechanic's set of coveralls, his chest hair spilling out of the slightly pulled down zipper. He had rolled the sleeves of it up to his elbows, which meant he was very serious about the project he was deep in currently. Though he was small statured, he was solid and strong, but lifting engines and generators would do that. I felt his grasp around my middle loosen a bit, but then felt his sweaty face press into my chest.

"Some days it's good to be short." He laughed as I pushed him away and shook my head.

" Your fiancée would agree with you old dog." I kissed the top of his head and let him go. Grabbing the white sheet bundle from the back of the bicycle. "I finished up the skin, I thought I would drop it by now that I don't have the Sheriff, hopefully, watching my every move."

I handed over the bundle, and Sal smiled brightly under his mustache. He gestured for me to follow him into the well kept garage. He was always pretty neat and tidy, even if everything was a little old and grease stained in the shop. Sal plopped the sheet down on the workbench and hurriedly unwrapped it. The deep brown fur of the bear skin exposed, he buried his face into it and took a deep breath. A satisfied sigh came from him, he stayed for several seconds taking in the scent and feel of the creatures warm fur.

"It's perfect Tailen. Thank you." The sound of his voice was heavily muffled by the fibers. Finally coming up for air, he wrapped it back in the white sheet. " Marcella will be able to make something beautiful with this, I'm so pleased."

"Glad to hear it, friend." I found a spot to sit down on some tires. They squished slightly more than I liked under my weight, and I had to catch myself from slipping back into the hole in the center. Maybe not my best idea, but I found balance by planting my feet on the hard paint splattered concrete floor.

Sal leaned on the table facing me, his arms crossed loosely over his chest. I had already reached into the leather satchel I placed on my lap, rummaging around.

"That Federal Agent came down here asking about Frank. Since they found him here and all. Apparently the deputy didn't take good enough notes for his liking. Seemed like he was pretty irritated by having to 'chase down' leads." His voice quivered slightly when he mentioned Frank's name. They had been close. "I told him all I knew, since I gave Frank the apartment above the shop when me and Marcella moved out I never really bothered to go up there, I let him go have a look around, see if he could find anything helpful."

Finally finding what I was looking for, I pulled a long thin wooden pipe from my bag. The neck of the pipe was long and skinny, sloping downwards towards the bowl, the wood carved with scarring writing patterns, inlaid with a jade stone. Poking some of a bright green leaf down into the bowl, I packed it tightly with my smallest finger. Giving it a small test draw before offering it to Sal. Who nodded quietly and took it.

"I'm really sorry that I wasn't there Sal, I'm really sorry about Frank." I set my bag down on the floor. " We both knew something was not normal after the second murder, I wish it hadn't hit you so close to home." Sal found a lighter in his coveralls pocket, and lit the pipe, taking a long hard drag off the stem. He held it and let it out after a moment.

A dull green smoke wafted up around his head, swirling in the stale air of the garage. As he exhaled the smoke was more of a deep forest green, and seemed to fall straight to the floor pooling around his heavy booted feet. It smelled sweet and earthy, like the forest floor after a heavy rain,

"He was just getting his feet back under him. Looking for work other than helping me. Trying to figure out where to go with himself. It's just....It just ain't right Tailen." He sniffed a little and handed the pipe back to me. The last of the smoke left his lips as he spoke.

"Maybe this agent will listen to the evidence in front of him. Now that he's here, maybe I will actually be able to get some answers, we can get those people some justice." I paused for a moment, gauging Sal's face before proceeding with my question. "Would you be able to tell me about the day you found Frank?"

I took a long drag on the pipe in my hand. The smoke filled my chest and sinuses. The calm that washed over my body is hard to describe. It's like sitting in a warm bath full of the best salts and oils a person could buy. Like looking into the sky at the eye of a storm over the ocean. Not ecstasy, but serenity of the body. The deep green smoke as I exhaled traveled down my chest and hit the floor, spreading out like a fog in off the lake shore on an autumn morning.

"I can try." Sal shifted on his feet a little taking the pipe back. "I found him in the back of the shop, like he was taking a nap on the old couch back there, but he didn't stir when I called his name. I'm angry with myself for thinking that he passed out from drinking again now ...but at the time, that's what I thought." His face shifted, his lips downturned as he continued to speak. " He wasn't though, once I touched his arm to wake him, he was cold. Colder than he should have been, I shook him for a good minute before..."

I stood up and went to my friend, placing my hand on his arm, sliding down to take his, squeezing. He nodded and kept speaking.

"At least his eyes were closed, but he had a burn, just like the others, his was on his neck. We both know that burn Tailen. I know you weren't too sure seeing it from far away, but up close, there is no misunderstanding."

"A spirit."

"Had to have been. Him being that cold, with that kind of wound, it would have to be someone really nasty." He breathed slowly, and started to recompose himself. Though I could see the tears forming.

"There can't be many here that would be able to, all the iron in the ground, but why now?"

"Marcella said she would do some research at work, see if she could dig anything up in the town history. We all know they like to try and hide that behind the new town name and all the flashy road signs." Marcella was always super busy with her work, so it would be on me to do it. Which I did not mind in the least.

"We will figure out who did this, Sal. I promise. For Frank, and for the rest of those people." I gripped his hand tightly again and stood back giving him a little space to wipe his face off. " Did Agent Lewis find anything up in his room that might have been helpful?"

"Not that he shared. Like I said he seemed pretty irritated, smelled like he had been at the cemetery or the morgue recently, maybe that has something to do with it, I know that coroner isn't exactly the most fun to deal with."

"A cemetery? Like the southside one?"

"Yeah, come to think of it, he smelled like lavender. Why?"

"I gave him Harold's name. So I guess he does follow leads without much thought."

"Why on earth did you send him looking for that Spirit? Harold didn't do all this, he's not even strong enough to get out of the cemetery." Sal looked a little unamused.

"I wanted to see what he would do with the information, see if he was a believer or not. You know how most people are. They deny the existence of what does not fit their status quo. The Unknowns." I gestured with air quotes.

The Unknowns is what a lot of United States government agencies refer to supernatural and metaphysical occurrences as. As scientific advancement happened it was as if people just forgot, which in some respects was good. It kept non-humans safe for the most part. They could hide in plain sight, just living their lives alongside their human counterparts. It was only sometimes when things like spirits got out of hand, and had to be delt with.

Sal sighed, nodding along with my logic. If I could get some eyes on one of the spirits that the police like to deny, then maybe there wouldn't be any more unnecessary death in the community. I hiked my bag up on my shoulder.

"I'm going to head to the library, maybe if I dig up a good enough lead, he will investigate our suspicions. Are you going to be okay if I head down? Want me to have Marcella come be with you?" By this point he was walking me back to my trike.

"I'll be alright for now, that smoke will tide me over for the afternoon, I might need to go have a nice walk in the woods this evening though ...would be nice to get out of these coveralls and feel the wind in my hair." He patted my back as I hopped on the bike seat and settled my feet down on the pedals.

I kissed his cheek goodbye as I headed in towards the town square.

It wasn't a far ride from his shop into the town proper, it took me past a couple of the badly pun named souvenir stores, and through a small amount of traffic that the coming weekend was bringing in.

The familiar sight of the dark SUV that was in my gravel drive a few days earlier, parked in front of *Rose's Café*. He had figured out that her donuts were the best in town pretty quickly I guess. Hopefully she hadn't sunk her claws into him too much, though honestly resisting her charms would be extremely hard. I chuckled to myself quietly as I parked my bike in front of the large library. I could already feel the looming presence of knowledge that hung in its old walls.

Looking over to the side of the door at the community board, I noted the growing amount of new advertising since the last time I was here. It wasn't like Marcella to let it get too crowded. So I pulled a few things down that seemed old. A worn out ad for the gas station's new lottery counter, a torn lost pet sign, a bright orange Help Wanted sign, and a few tattered business cards. I rearranged what was left, making sure you could see everything more clearly. That felt much better. I folded and shoved the rest of the papers down into my satchel.

I pulled the heavy iron and glass door to the library open, and headed inside. My goal was heading down into the archives in the basement, because I had some reading to do.

I thought I heard my name being yelled as the door closed behind me.

Chapter 4

Mikhail

"Well hello Sugar! How are you?" The bubbling voice of Rose wasn't exactly comforting this afternoon. I'm sure the day's annoyance could be read all over my face, though it seemed to not phase her one bit.

"Considering I have spent the last couple days chasing dead ends, 'Fine' would be a rather dishonest answer."

"I'm sorry to hear that Sugar." Rose's face turned to a rather pouty one and felt a bit patronizing to be honest. "How about I get you a strong coffee and a jelly donut? That always makes me feel much better."

"I'll take it to go please. I have to go back to the station and make sure they have faxed everything over to the main office. They are not exactly efficient over there."

I had foregone the suit jacket and tie today leaving my top two buttons undone, as it was pretty hot outside. The beginning of summer sun is starting to make me regret having a job that required such a stodgy uniform. Scanning the cafe as she got my coffee together, the place was pretty busy, though there were a few empty booths. It was in my scanning that I saw a familiar figure ride by on an old tricycle out the big front windows. I felt my blood start to turn hot as she passed by.

Miss Galloway has sent me on a bad lead, and she had done it on purpose. The rising anger in my gut made me forget about the coffee that Rose was preparing for me and I made a quick bee line towards the street. The door of the cafe jingled loudly as I threw the door open and walked quickly out onto the sidewalk. I heard Rose cuss a little as she realized I left. I would probably have to deal with that later .

"Miss Galloway!" I yelled after her, but it seemed she didn't hear me. I adjusted my belt that held my badge, gun, and pager, then looked both ways as I crossed the street heading towards the town center. Where was she going? She was pretty far ahead of me at this point, so I picked up my speed. Walking quickly around the people on the sidewalk stopped to admire the old trees on the lawn of the courthouse. I could see her park the old trike in front of the large library.

"TAILEN GALLOWAY." My voice rose in volume significantly, she didn't seem to react, even though it did turn the heads of other people in the street. Was she ignoring me? She had to have heard me at this point but kept walking inside the building. The people of this town already had a way of getting on my nerves. I huffed as I opened the doors of the library. Who makes the doors of a public building this heavy to open?

The library was one of the oldest buildings in town, and looked like it. Hailing from the earlier days of the town, it was a converted church. It towered over even the court-house, making it not only one of the oldest, but tallest buildings in the town. The stonework of the walls was held in place by iron beams. It spoke to the beginnings of the town of the past being known for its iron working. The inside was cathedral like, what would have been stone in a normal city, was iron work here. Decorative scrawling pillars, even the stained glass being held in place with thin precise metal work of the same ilk. Being renovated into a library meant that it had a large central desk, and wooden bookshelves lined the walls and created aisles and nooks where one could sit on couches and at tables to read. Seemed strange in a town so small like this, to have such a fine library. It was clear that at some point a person cared enough to make it a comfortable place for knowledge in the tourism laden town.

The black haired woman I was chasing was nowhere to be found. She must have ducked into one of the aisles. As I made my way across the hard stone floor, a woman looked up from the central desk. The name plate made of glinting bronze said, Marcella DeLance- Head Librarian.

"Hello! How can I help you today?" The woman's voice was clear, and had a twinge of a New Orleans accent in her tone.

She was average height, deep brown skin tone. Her face had rounded features and vibrant honey colored eyes behind large round silver rimmed glasses. The large loose curly afro bounced as she continued to work scanning books on the desk while she spoke. She had on a summer dress that was green, and looked bright against her dark skin, bare arms held barely visible tattooing in black ink.

I caught my breath from my jog across the center of town. Placing a hand on the wooden desk, to steady myself.

"Did you see Miss Galloway come past here?" My tone was harsher than I had meant; Which caused the smile from her face to fall and a furrowed brow to take its place.

"And who wants to know?" One of her thin eyebrows cocked, defensiveness in her voice as she crossed her arms.

"I'm Agent Lewis, FBI. I need to ask her a few questions." I gestured to the badge that was tucked around the front of my belt. Adjusting my tone. "If you would tell me where she went, I would appreciate it Ma'am."

"Hm. Fine, she headed down to the basement archives. You better be on your best behavior down there. The books are delicate and old. Don't give me a reason to ask you to leave." That sounded more like a threat than her merely doing her job, but I nodded in agreement. I wasn't interested in bothering with the book collection. I just wanted to confront the woman who sent me on a wild goose chase across town.

Marcella gestured towards the right side of the library, there was an alcove to that side that had a set of iron stairs that lead downwards. She quietly went back to scanning the books and stacking them neatly on a cart.

As I headed down the stairs, my heavy foot falls causing the metal stairs to reverberate against the walls louder than i anticipated. The air felt colder as I went down, the natural light of the windows in the main part of the library waning, and making way to the overhead dimmer sepia toned lights of the basement.

The rows of shelves down here were broken up by glass cases, holding what seemed to be artifacts from the town, as well as a large topographic table map of the town dated many decades before. It was more spread out down here than it was upstairs. Tables had small lamps on them so one could easily read the old texts while sitting at them. The air was strongly scented, like cedar and leather, though a hint of mildew could be caught in the far reaches of the large underground room.

"Miss Galloway." I sternly called her name. It bounced off the walls, and I heard shuffling from the next row of book-cases. My steps were heavy and urgent as I hurriedly walked towards the noise. As I stepped into the space between the shelves I was greeted by the back of her head. She was in fact ignoring me. "MISS GALLOWAY."

"Shhhh. Lower your voice Agent Lewis. Respect the library." I heard a book snap shut as she turned around and faced me. Those deep brown eyes narrowed slightly, her straight thin black eyebrows pushed together forming a wrinkle in the middle of her forehead.

"You have a lot of nerve telling me...."

"I said...lower your voice" her tone matched mine, but was quieter, almost a hiss as it escaped her lips. Still having trouble placing her accent. Maybe Welsh? I puffed myself up a bit in a defensive manner. Lowering the volume before speaking again.

"You have a lot of never telling me what to do. I should arrest you for obstructing an investigation after the stunt you pulled."

"What did I do Agent Lewis?" Her eyes shifted back to the book shelves, tipping the book in her hand back into its place between two others. "All I did was give you a name."

"You made me look like an idiot. Sent me to question a dead man."

"I did, but Harold isn't too bad of a guy, for being dead and all."

I slammed my hand against the hard wooden bookcase and pointed my finger at her taking a small step towards her.

"Those fuckers at the police station probably got a real laugh at my expense, I spent an hour trying to track the address they gave me down to a house, because you thought you would try and pull one over on me. Maybe I was wrong about you being innocent."

Tailen's eyes flicked back to me and reached up mindlessly grabbing a larger leather bound book. Pulling it down into her chest.

"Well that's not completely my fault then is it?" A sly smile spread across her lips as she literally pushed past me heading towards one of the tables, her shoulder hitting mine was a lot stronger than someone her stature should have been. "Did old Harold have anything good to say anyway?"

I spun around following close on her heels. Walk away from me in the middle of a conversation, how rude.

"What do you mean! It was a gravestone. There was no one there. You should know, you started me down that ridiculous lead."

She looked up from the book she had opened on the table, and seemed confused. Her head cocked to one side, hair flipping over as she did.

"What? He should have been there. Harold can't leave the cemetery. He's always there. Floating about, complaining about the chipmunks. Not that you can hear him, his spirit is not strong enough for that."

I threw my hands up in the air. Now she was talking about spirits. Like those quacks down in the Unknowns Department.

"You have to be joking. Spirits? Now you're going to talk about spirits? You think, I came all the way out to this podunk tourist town to talk to someone from beyond the grave. Maybe I should take you in." My anger was subsiding at this point, it had turned to exasperated irritation.

"Yes, Spirits ...wait, was he really not there?" This actually seemed to worry her, she sat down, on the edge of the table, crossing her arms over her chest, her head shaking.

"I don't know who you think I am Miss Galloway, but I'm not buying you sent me to talk to a spirit and he wasn't there. It's just a crock that people like to spew when they don't want to take the blame for something." I place my hand on the table next to her. I was probably closer than I should have been, but I was not happy and if she wasn't going to listen, using a bit of intimidation may help. "Now I think you're hiding something."

"So you're one of the deniers." Her face turned towards mine, it had gone blank. Though up this close, I could see into her eyes, there was a fierceness behind them. "Fine, but you can't deny the physical evidence on the bodies. By now you have to have read the coroner's reports right?"

"What does that have to do with spirits?" I could feel her breath on my face as she sighed and rolled her eyes.

"The burns. They are clearly from a spirit coming in contact with the victims. Didn't they teach you this shit in your training? Did they send a rookie to handle a serial murder case." She knew she was pushing my buttons, and she was very clearly not backing down.

I stepped away, rubbing the back of my head and growling under my breath. Trying to hold back the growing urge to yell. It wasn't easy, my temper got the best of me sometimes and I was trying very hard to keep it under wraps.

"Those have not been identified yet, and there is no evidence to suggest...."

"It's bullshit and you know it. You're just not looking at it the right way, it's not my fault you want to deny hard evidence. In your line of work...there is no..."

My hand slammed against the side of one of the heavy bookcases. It rattled slightly, the sound of the smack cut off Tailen's words. I balled up my fist against the wood.

"You are distracting me from the case Miss Galloway." My tone was cool, as I pushed down the urge to snap back harshly. "This is not a case of a spirit going on a killing spree....because they don't do ..."

I stopped speaking because the air that was leaving my mouth turned to a puff of visible vapor in front of my face. I could see my breath coming from my nose as well, the chill of the air deepened. I looked at Tailen and her breath was the same. I looked down at my feet, a couple of small books had fallen off the shelf, when I had slammed my hand into it, landing on the stone floor.

"Well, you're not going to be able to deny this one Agent." She had a look of satisfaction on her face, lip curled up on one side in a smirk. I looked past her as the lights on the tables began to shudder slightly, and the overheads completely went out.

From the other end of the basement I could hear loud clicking steps, like that of high heeled shoes. The sound grew closer, and as it did a woman's figure formed from nothing. Looking at her was like looking at a projected image. The movements were not smooth, like a stop motion animation, but the sounds that the woman made were. The footsteps and the rustling of the dress she wore were all clear as a church bell. She didn't have many features that I could make out, but the silhouette looked like a woman from the 1950's in a shirtwaist dress, her hair pulled back into a high bun on her head.

I would be lying to say I wasn't shocked, spirits didn't just manifest on cue. No, no this wasn't happening. I stepped away as she got closer, and the closer she got to me, the colder I felt. It was almost painful. As she stepped through the table and past Tailen, the spirit bent down, picking up the books that fell, carefully placing them back on the end of the shelf.

"Who.....who is what..." I stammered without meaning to. Trying to push some repressed memories back, as seeing this woman was bringing up things I didn't want to think about. A memory of screaming and the feel of cold entering my mind.

"This is Mrs. Bea. She started the library. When she died she asked to be buried down here. I don't think she realized that she would be stuck shelving books for the rest of existence, but here she is." Miss Galloway seemed calm now, almost comforted by telling me this.

"I'm not following. The Unknowns Department says spirits only stay if they have unresolved shit." I was trying really hard at this point to keep the old thoughts buried. Those memories were blurry and I liked them to stay that way.

"Oh, that's because of the iron in the building. She can't get out. Someone would have to move her actual body for her to be able to move on or manifest anywhere else, and in this town with all the iron in the ground, she would just be unhappy that she wasn't where she wanted to be." Pushing herself up from leaning, she dropped her hands to her hips. "You ready to listen to what I have to say Agent Lewis, or are we going to continue arguing?"

"I'm now at a loss." I took a step towards the spirit, reaching a hand towards her I could feel the cold radiating off her. It was almost like putting my hand over dry ice.

"You dumb...what are you doing." Tailen jumped forward grabbing my hand forcefully yanking me away, and breaking my gaze on the spirit of Bea. She gripped my wrist with more force than I would have thought she could apply. "I told you just five minutes ago that I believed there were spirit burns on the murder victims and now you want to touch one?"

"I wasn't thinking." My hand did feel really cold, like I had dunked it in an ice bath, and the cold lingered even as we watched the spirit dissipate into nothingness, having completed her task as the overhead lights flickered back on. Tailen put both her hands around mine, the warmth of her skin starting to thaw my cold fingers.

"I'm going to ask you again. Do you want to hear what I have to say or are you going to keep denying what may be the truth?" Her eyes stared into mine, her hands rubbing my cold fingers as she did. I pinched my nose bridge with my free hand and with defeat in my voice I acquiesced.

"Fine. I will listen. As long as you don't send me across town to embarrass me again. I have enough drama to deal with talking to Sheriff Southland."

"I'm glad to hear it. I can go back to liking you again Agent, instead of wanting to toss you through a bookcase."

"Then I would have to arrest you for assaulting a Federal officer..." That came out a lot flatter than I had intended.

Tailen unwrapped her hands from around mine, pulling it up closer to her face, seemingly to check that it wasn't burned. When she looked satisfied she lowered it back down.

"Just remember to not let them touch you. A little bit will just burn, too long and it will stop your heart." She returned to the book on the table, hopping up this time, sitting on the table pulling the book onto her lap.

"I'll try to remember that...is everyone in town aware that there is a spirit here? Or ...."

" Oh, most people know, they just ignore it. Like some people do rats or stray dogs. It's more of a nuisance to them to think about than actually dealing with the fact they may end up like that. Most people don't like to think about their mortality."

Oof, that last sentence hit a little harder than I liked. Between that and battlefield memories that were creeping into the back of my head, I wasn't going to sleep well tonight.

"I'm guessing that your reading has something to do with what you want to tell me Miss Galloway."

"It's Tailen, I'm not telling you again, and yes. Sort of. I am sure that a spirit is doing the killing, but because the bodies were dumped, and not where they were killed, it would have to be someone with a rather powerful spirit. This book has a list and family details of all the most powerful families that have been in the town since it was founded." She gestured for me to come look, I leaned against the table next to her, placing a hand behind her, leaning so I could see the book as she turned the page. The smell of old musty books hit my nostrils. I sniffled a little bit.

"And you think one of these people is responsible for killing someone....now?" I still found that hard to believe but reached over, turning to the next page myself, my eyes trailing across the old printing, seeing if anything caught my eye.

"There were a lot of deaths when this place was a mining town, a spirit could be hanging onto some of the resentment, and finally got enough juice to do something about it." I watched as her fingers trailed across the pages for a few moments. However as she turned one page, it grazed across the front of her shirt, which caught my attention, and I caught myself looking at the rather perky hard nipples that could be seen from under her shirt. Of course she wasn't wearing a bra.

The rising tension of the argument had gotten my brain all a mess, and now I felt myself unable to pull my gaze from her chest. What kind of messed up person am I to think that it was an appropriate thing to be doing at this moment. I closed my eyes and tried to focus back down on the pages, but she closed the book with a bit of a snap.

"You know, it's perfectly natural when a person gets worked up by an argument to need somewhere to put that energy Agent Lewis." Her lips were close to my ear, I could feel her warm breath on my ear lobe. It made me feel even weaker than I already did at the moment.

" Tailen, I'm not 'worked' up. I'm just tired. All of this new... .information is....a lot. I have to reevaluate the evidence and make some calls and...." I could feel her shifting on the table the sound of her boots hitting the floor. She was standing in front of me now, one of her boots planted between my feet. I opened my eyes, looking at the floor in an attempt to fight back the intrusive thoughts.

"Then, we have a lot of work to do, Agent." Her body leaned forward into mine, one of her hands placed gently on my chest just below where my shirt was unbuttoned. "How about this ...I gather more information from here. You go make your calls....and I will meet you tomorrow at your motel, and I'll bring the coffee."

The urge to grab her waist was almost unmanageable. I wanted to wrap my arms around her soft warm middle and bury my face into her neck. I knew there was too much going on in my mind, and I wasn't going to make the mistake of doing something I shouldn't. Even though I was getting a very clear invitation.

"I will see you tomorrow then Tailen...." I averted my eyes to the side, and I could see her face fall just a little bit. She however pushed away from my chest and stood up straight. She grabbed the book from the table and nodded to me as she headed back down through the shelves.

"Tomorrow Misha." She waved over her head. When had I told her my name? Let alone...know the moniker my grandmother called me.

I felt my face flush.

I'm not going to make it out of this town in one piece.

Chapter 5

Tailen

I knew I was pushing my luck, teasing that poor man so much. I spoke from my own body's reaction when I said it was normal to get 'worked up' after an argument. Just the rush of emotion was a lot for me, though I should have taken it into consideration that I tend to feel things more than others. To cool myself off, I wandered back down between the heavy bookcases, running a hand down the spines of books on the shelves. I could hear Mikhail's heavy steps as he headed back up the iron stairs to the main lobby of the library.

I spent quite some time poking around in the books, looking for any handwritten logs or ledgers. One name kept coming up in most of the older books. A family name, Neisbeith. They seemed to be the owners of most of the mines and one of the largest iron works. That place was out on the eastern side of the lake, if I recall correctly. I never found a reason to go out there, though I did enjoy looking through abandoned buildings. None of factories or offices had been in working order for a very long time. There were probably very few people left in the town that remembered them even being open. I know there had been some sort of mine collapse. Maybe that was related to all this somehow? Maybe not.

I gathered the books I wanted to take with me, any on the old families that had members murdered, ledgers from the old courthouse, a folded map of the old town, and a couple binders of old news clippings. They all seemed relevant to my theory. Hopefully with the evidence from the police and Mikhail, we will be able to make some headway on the murder cases. The time was getting on, and the evening sun was descending almost below the stained glass windows, casting beautiful patterns of light onto the stone floors and iron pillars. I could spend an inordinate amount of time just watching those dancing beams.

I stacked the books together, heading up the stairs to the central desk, plopping the stack down on the counter, look-ing around it, and locking eyes with Marcella. Who didn't look all too pleased with me.

"What did you do to that man, Tailen? He left here red-faced and looking like a teenage boy who just had been caught doing something naughty."

"We argued, he met Mrs. Bea, he agreed to re-examine evi-dence with a new lens. Which...is why I need all these books." I patted the top of the stack and then leaned both elbows down on the counter, placing my head on my fists. Watching as she opened and scanned each book.

"I shouldn't be letting you take some of these Tailen. I know you will bring them back in one piece." She reached under the desk when she finished scanning, grabbing a file box and stacking the books down into it. "I know you're going to take them on your bike, this should fit in that basket of yours." Marcella patted the top of the box to seal the lid tight. "Did you go see Sal?"

"I dropped off the bear pelt. He seemed pleased with it. We talked about Frank briefly. He mentioned maybe going on a walk tonight." I pulled the box off the counter, and leaned over the desk, accepting a cheek kiss and returning it to my friend.

"I may have to join him then." She pulled the chain switch of the light on her desk. "Just have to finish up here. You keep that Agent Lewis safe if you're going to be looking for spirits."

I gave her a hard nod as I hoisted the box of books up on my shoulder, heading back outside to get loaded up onto my trike. The streets of the town had settled a bit as the evening came on, the restaurants were full of people as I rode through town. Most of the tourists would have headed out to their cabins and camping sites for the evening. You could see small billows of smoke coming up from around the lake area, and the surrounding woods from campfires. The one thing that the local police had done was keep the murders under wraps. It hadn't seemed to affect the tourism that was the life blood of this town.

I took the long way home, taking the route through the woods, which was calm. It smelled like heavy pine, and I could just hear a wolf's howl on the wind.

The morning came swifter than I thought having spent most of the night listening to music and going through the journals and books I brought home. I had found some relevant information that I would have to share with Agent Lewis, though I still couldn't figure out why now that if a spirit was manifesting, what the reason would be. Perhaps someone was angry that the town had forgotten its roots? Some spirits get bent out of shape for the strangest things. Especially ones that can't go anywhere. Which in this town, surrounded by literal mountains of iron, and spirits had a hard time doing much of anything, which is why I'm so invested in who it could be.

I leaned out the window, looking into the woods behind my cabin, taking a long drag on my pipe. Letting the smoke spill down the ground in a long swirling stream. I watched a few birds twiddling in the air. It was always fascinating to me to watch small animals existing and living in their natural spaces. Life was simple for them. Not so much for the rest of us.

I dressed simply as I usually did for the heat, and packed my satchel with my pipe. Though I doubt that it would be needed. I had washed my hair in the shower this morning, so it was staying slicked back the way I combed it. I made sure to grab the box as I headed out; I would have to remember to stop at Rose's to grab the coffee that I had promised. I have a feeling that my bribe of coffee was part of the reason he agreed to let me help.

The ride to town was uneventful, town was bustling and busy as the weekend had now hit. I could hear the voices of hiking guides using megaphones to try and gather their groups efficiently in the town center. The restaurants were busy as ever, though I knew Rose would have at least enough time to get me a couple of coffees to take with me to meet Mikhail. I pulled my tricycle up onto the sidewalk and parked it up against the pink building. I made sure the box was still secured in the basket, and headed into the busy cafe.

"Good morning Rose." I approached the counter, and leaned down on it with my elbows.

"Oh it is in fact a good morning. Would be better if you could tell me why that Agent decided he needed to take off before he got his coffee yesterday chasing after your bike." Rose's accent was always a bit thicker when she was irritated with me, as if him taking off across the street was actually my fault. Maybe it was. It in fact was my fault.

"I didn't know he chased me from here. He was angry with me, but it's been resolved now. I'm heading to see him, and I promised Agent Lewis coffee. No hard feelings from him I hope." I would hope not at least, considering he agreed to let me help.

"I mean, I wouldn't mind a hard feeling from that one if I were you, Tailen, but that's just me." Rose poured coffee for a man at the counter as she spoke to me, and his face turned red at her innuendo. Rose winked at him and turned to grab some paper to go cups for me.

"Let's be honest Rose, you wouldn't mind a hard feeling from most people in a suit and tie." I heard the man who she winked at almost spit out his coffee. Which caused Rose to start laughing, which just like everything else about her was perfect and infectious. She set my coffees down in front of me, and also a bag with something sweet smelling inside.

"You let him know running out on a lady like he did yesterday is completely unacceptable, and I won't let it happen again. I made his coffee with extra cream and sugar, you be sure to give him the right one." Rose gave me an air kiss as she shuffled off down the counter to continue serving the patrons who were all now more interested than they even were before making it apparent she was thirsty for something more than coffee.

I'm glad for the basket on the back of my trike, otherwise getting both drinks and this bag of pastries to the other side of town would have been much harder. I now understood why people drive cars. I was never interested in learning to drive one of those machines. I found my way back out into the street. Luckily once out of the town center, I didn't have to fight against any traffic. I was glad for the fading sound of town, and the calming feel of the wind and sounds of the lake overtaking the air, and I could smell the water. The western shore of the lake was close-ish to the motel where the agent was staying. It wasn't the only one in town, but it was the only one that was worth staying in. I actually had stayed here for my first month in town years ago. I helped do repairs and cleaning in exchange for room and board.

I rode around the building until I found the vehicle belonging to the Agent. As I pulled my bike up onto the sidewalk in front of the building I could hear Mikhail's voice coming from inside the nearest unit. So grabbing the coffees and pastry bag, I balanced them on top of the file box containing the books. I used my foot to kick the door, since my hands were full. I heard shuffling and then the sound of what I assumed was the phone falling to the floor, cussing and finally the sound of the dead bolt being unlocked.

I was greeted by a rather sleepy looking man. Agent Lewis looked as if he hadn't slept well, I hoped I didn't have a part to play in that. His face was unshaven, but he looked like he was wearing clean clothing. The black pants, and a dark blue shirt, unbuttoned the same as it was yesterday. He, however, hadn't bothered putting shoes on, and I didn't blame him. I only wore mine because it wasn't socially acceptable to just walk around in my bare feet all the time. I nodded my head towards the coffee that was his. He grabbed it and took a long deep sip from the cup before he even said anything to me.

" Mornin' Miss...." My eyes narrowed at him as he spoke. " Tailen, Yes. Good morning. Thanks." He stood back holding the door open, giving me the opportunity to brush past him and into the rather dimly lit room, which I didn't mind. I noticed he has turned all the lamps on, and hasn't flipped the main switch for the overhead lights. I wouldn't be changing that.

Setting the box down on the floor next to the table, I looked around noticing that he had case files spread out on the table, the small counter that held the unused coffee pot, and any other surface in the room that he could. Welp, not what I would call organized, but if it worked for him....then I suppose it would have to do. I was hoping he had a starting place. I heard him plunk down hard in one of the chairs at the table, setting his coffee down and rubbing his face.

"You look like you didn't get much sleep last night, Agent. I hope your insomnia proved fruitful?" I squatted down next to my box, moving the coffee and pastries to a clear spot on the table, and starting to pull the books out. Though I'm not sure where I am going to put them.

"No, I didn't. I fell asleep in the chair by the bed for a few hours. I spent a while last night on the phone with the Unknowns Department back at headquarters. I probably should have been nicer to them, it took some bribing to get them to agree to fax over any information they find about the town. Just to see if there has been any investigations here in the past." He started shuffling papers on the table around, stacking them so I could set the books down on it.

"Hopefully they are getting something good out of the deal then." I decided to get comfortable since it seemed as if we had some work to do. I tossed my bag down under the table, and pushed my boots off. Grabbing my coffee I took a swig and took one of the files from the top of the stack. " The coroner finally got himself in gear, and finished the autopsies?"

"His findings are all over the place. He is saying that the guy who had the gaping chest wound died from a stopped heart. I could have told him that, considering from the photos the man's organs were sitting on his lap." Mikhail looked frustrated, but at least he seemed to be waking up from drinking the coffee. "I've been looking at the particulates that were found on all the bodies. I'm not sure what help it is though, because it's all mostly iron and this town is full of that."

"He does seem to note the burns, at least he didn't skip over that, but he just puts an unknown cause. If all of the victims also have damage to the heart, it wouldn't surprise me. I told you, prolonged contact with a spirit can cause that to happen."

"I'm just still trying to wrap my head around that part of it honestly, but I'm coming up blank with anything else that supports a theory other than what you are suggesting."

"Mikhail, why don't you let me look through the files, you tuck into some of the books I brought, and get fresh eyes on both things. I would be interested to see what you find out on the Neisbeith family, that's who I have been focusing on."

"Sounds better than anything I have come up with in the last few hours." He eyed the bag of pastries that Rose had sent. I pushed them towards him across the table, and his eyes turned a bit greedy as he pulled one of the cream cheese Danishes out and started to devour it. Not only was he tired, but also apparently hungry.

That was the start of the day, every once in a while, I would pick up a new file while I paced around the room. On occasion one of us would chime in with something to look for in our respective texts, every time I finished with a file, I would stack it next to the coffee pot so that It would be out of the way.

After a few hours of this I found myself sitting on the floor reading though the last coroner's report, this one was Franks. Something I had noted throughout all four files, was the presence of fuel found on the clothing along with limestone and iron flecks. I recalled that one the name that kept coming up in the books owned both mines, and a smelting plant. I skimmed through, and even though the cause of death for Frank was listed as asphyxiation, it was noted there was trauma to the heart.

"Mikhail, do you have the evidence bags of Frank's effects? Sal mentioned...." I looked up from the file and noticed that my comrade was leaning forward in his chair, leaning on the arm. Blue eyes closed, his breathing gentle and rhythmic. Well, at least he was getting some sort of sleep. I closed the folder and pushed myself up off the floor. Quietly I set it down and walked over.

I reached gently to the sleeping man, he looked peaceful in the face. I let my fingers touch his hair, pushing it back from his brow, it was soft and even though it looked unkempt. I felt him rouse, and his eyes snapped open his hand grabbing my wrist. I had very much startled him awake. Wasn't my intention. It took him a second before he dropped my hand and rubbed his eyes.

"How long was I out for?" His voice sounded groggy.

"I'm not sure, I was stuck into Frank's file and noticed when I tried to ask a question. I didn't mean to startle you. If you're tired, we can pick this up tomorrow. It's not like the killer is going anywhere, we have all but confirmed my suspicions." I took a slight step back away from him, leaning a hand down onto the table.

"I'm fine, I just need more coffee, maybe something to eat…besides a couple of Danish." He stretched his arms over his head leaning back in the chair enough that I could hear the bones in his spine pop and crackle. "What were you doing anyway?"

"I was just trying to wake you gently, That's all." That was a lie, what I wanted was to touch his hair.

"You always seem to be getting into my space when I least expect it Tailen." He looked at me with those sleepy blue eyes, he didn't seem irritated when he spoke. It was more matter o' fact.

"This is the first time without being provocated by you looking at my body." I placed my hands on my hips, cocking them to one side, apparently him being tired, canceled out whatever filter he has had about it to this point.

"Even the first day we met, it's not like you hid it from me." His face turned a pink color at his cheeks. "And yesterday in that cold basement, it's not like your shirt left much to the imagination." I remember how the cold made my body react, getting goosebumps, hardening my nipples so they showed through the thin shirt.

"This conversation seems pointless Mikhail. We should just get back to work, or get you something to eat and pick this up tomorrow." I shook my head, and bent down grabbing my empty box. Meaning to pack up some of the books to take with me. That's when I heard the chair shift and felt a warm hand grab ahold of my arm, gently he pulled me back up to face him.

"I'm too tired to argue or keep my hands to myself." Mikhail's free hand wound its way around my middle, I could feel his large fingers touching the skin on my back just under the hem of my shirt. "You are driving me up a wall, Tailen. I shouldn't be distracted from the case, but I'm finding it hard to focus when you touch me."

"Distractions are not always a bad thing. Sometimes getting your mind off a daunting task can help refresh your view." I felt him pull me into him with the hand on my lower back, and the warmth of his breath as he buried his face into the crook of my neck. My arms were now pinned between us resting on his chest. I curled my fingers, body shuddering as I felt his tongue running up the side of my neck and him speaking into my ear in a low voice.

"The papers can wait until later. You are a more than welcome distraction." He pulled away from my ear, meeting my gaze. His free hand snaking into the back of my hair, I leaned up slightly to meet him. Our lips met with fervor. His lips felt soft, but pushed into mine hard. I was right about the tension of yesterday getting us both worked up. I turned my head slightly to the side, my hands sliding up his chest to the sides of his face, lips parting to feel his warm tongue pushing into my mouth. It had been a while since I felt another kiss me in this way. He tasted like coffee. It sent a ripple of pleasure through my body.

He pulled back, allowing for us to catch our breath for a few seconds. My mouth curled up into a sly smile, and even though his eyes were half closed I could see his energy was matching mine. I kissed him again pushing my body into him, I felt his feet shift, apparently I pushed a little too hard, and he had to fix his footing. It created a little bit of space between us, which allowed me to drop my hands from his face back to his chest that was breathing deeply now, I could feel his heart starting to beat quickly under my hand. This man absolutely pulled my mind away from the task at hand. Gently I looked over my shoulder at the bed, before gazing back at him.

I pulled him by his shirt backwards towards the bed, and as the back of my legs hit the edge of the mattress, he placed a hand on my shoulder, pushing me so I feel down onto the bed. I pushed the papers that were in the way out from under myself without much thought as to what they were. He gazed down at me as I stretched my arms up over my head, exposing my mid-section. I could hear the low rumble of a growl come from his throat. His face was quickly on my stomach, the wetness of his tongue licking at my flesh, from the band of my shorts all the way up to the center of my chest hands pushing my shirt up as he did. His mouth left my skin long enough to push the shirt up over my head and arms. I hurriedly tossed the thin shirt away. The weight of his knees hit the bed, one of them pushed right up between my legs resting against the outside of the crotch of my shorts. The pressure on my sensitive area made a moan escape from my lips, which seemed to perk Mikhail's interest, because he moved his knee against me again.

I could feel his eyes scanning my bare chest, a warm hand finding its way to my breast, taking it fully into the grasp of his fingers. His lips fell to mine again, his free hand helping brace himself on the bed. I could get my hands to his chest now, my fingers pulling at the buttons of the shirt, and pulling it to untuck it from his pants. My breathing grew heavy like his as the warm feeling of pleasure spread though my body. I managed to help free him from his shirt. I finally got a good look at the man's chest. He was fairly hairy, his core was strong, and I could feel the muscles under the soft layer of his stomach. It was a crime itself that he hid this under his ill fitting clothing.

" Mikhail...." I called his name quietly, his mouth now having found my breast, tongue flicking at my hard nipple, my hips lifted in a slow rhythm against his knee, using his thigh to continue allowing myself to feel the pleasure of the pressure he was applying. I wanted to taste him, like he was me. I pulled his face away from my breast; as good as it felt I needed him on my lips. He obliged me without complaint. His fingers pinched my nipple between, which drew a hard moan out of me and broke the connection between our lips.

"You were not exaggerating about being worked up. You are sensitive...." His voice was quiet, the tone low. " and I can't wait to taste more of you." My face flushed red, and he smirked this time. I felt his body lower into me a bit, and I could feel the stiffness of his manhood now resting on my thigh. It was making his pants tight, and they pulled at the crotch. My growing anticipation was palpable. The wetness between my thighs threated to soak though my shorts.

However, he would not get his wish to taste more of me, because there was a knock at the door.

Of course there was a knock at the door.

Why wouldn't there be.

Chapter 6

Mikhail

Tailen's skin was so hot under my hands. My brain was filled with nothing but focus on her heavily breathing body below me. Her soft skin, her breasts, Even the large scar on the side of her torso was just so enticing. I really had needed to pull my mind away from the case, and her pressing herself into me yesterday was part of the reason I couldn't sleep last night, and attempted to busy myself with the files that were strewn all over the room.

The taste of her lingered on my lips, I greedily wanted to put them on every curve of her soft form. The growing tightness in my pants now pressed against her thigh as my hands started to reach under the small of her back, I wanted to remove those infuriating shorts she wore.

The universe had other ideas, and I was brought back to reality by the hard knock at the door. I was half tempted to let it go, let the knocking continue until they got bored. Keep immersing myself in her pleasant scent and flesh. I had to pull myself away because...I was still working. I groaned in annoyance and pushed off the bed, though not without glancing back at the heavily breathing woman lying shirtless on my bed. I didn't even grab my shirt as I went to open the door.

"What?" I threw the door open angrily. Grabbing it before it hit the wall. Which caused a loud smacking noise against my hand, and it stung. It was the lady from the front desk of the motel. She took a step back at my harsh tone. I took a deep breath and centered myself for a second. "I'm sorry.....What can I do for you ma'am?"

"Sorry to bother you Agent Lewis, but your office called the front desk, they said they tried your phone but it was just getting a busy signal. I thought it was important....." I nodded and tried to make myself look more pleasant in the face.

"Thank you, I must have left it off the hook by accident, I will give them a call back." She gave me a nod and apologized again. I shut the door and leaned back against it. Taking in a deep heavy breath, and letting out a long exasperated sigh. "Looks like work never ends."

Tailen had rolled over on her stomach, laying with her head on her arms, looking at me while also trying to catch her breath. She didn't seem as annoyed as I was. I went to the night stand and grabbed the phone. It had been still off the hook; I must not have seated it properly when I hung up with the office several hours ago. I sat down on the edge of the bed and looked back at her.

"I'm guessing the Unknowns Department tried calling, I should get back with them. I'm not trying to push my luck with them being cooperative." Tailen nodded and sort of shrugged as she laid her head down, looking at me. I could finally see the huge tattoo that took up most of her back now, I had never seen anything quite like that. It took up most of her torso, circular sigil-like markings. I couldn't read any of the characters that made up the writings around the edges, it was intricate weave of lines and symbols; and looked as if it has been done recently. Not dissimilar to the others that were on her shoulders, arms and legs. I was becoming increasingly aware that she was more than just a woman who lived in a cabin in the woods.

"I can gather my things in a moment. Go ahead and make your call. I just need to...calm myself down before I get up."

I tore my eyes away from her and picked up the receiver of the phone. I knew the number for the main line without thinking. I had to have the call redirected because I couldn't however remember the extension for the Unknowns department. It rang for a lot longer than I would have wanted before it got picked up.

"This is Agent Lewis, did you find anything worth sending over?.....Yeah, that's not much, can you fax it over to the station in the morning?.......I know it's the weekend. It can't wait until Monday...." I feel like they are just trying to be annoying at this point. Rolling my eyes I felt like tossing the whole phone out the window. "Yes I will get the department dinner for working tomorrow, just get the damn file sent. Thank you." I set the receiver down on the yellowed base, I could hear the crunch of the plastic as I let it go from me holding it so tightly.

Tailen had rolled over and found her shirt and was currently slipping it back over her head; the distraction was good while it lasted. I laid back on the bed covering my face with my hands.

"They found a record from back in the 60's. Apparently there was some sort of mine collapse. The bureau was here with a lot of other agencies for investigation and damage control. They will get it to me in the morning." I was reminded that there was work to be done. The stresses of the case flooded back into my mind. I felt the touch of her fingers on my hair, then the warm skin of her lips press against my forehead.

"Then we will resume in the morning. I want to take a look at the personal effects bags from the victims, and I'm not sure they are in the one box of case files they gave you at the station." Her fingers stayed in my hair for a few moments longer before I felt her weight lift from the mattress. "If you want out of this old hotel room, I'm happy to offer you respite at my cabin Agent Lewis."

Her calling me that felt strange, I didn't care for it. Now I know how she felt about her name. I could hear her rustling with her own box, though she didn't pack all the books back in it, I noticed she took the one with news articles and property logs. She must have gone back into work mode as well. I sat myself up slowly, and heard my stomach rumble, the ache of not having had proper food set in.

"I think that would be good, this room is starting to annoy me. I will come by in the morning, hopefully what they are sending will clear up the road block we have hit." I watched as she tugged on her boots, the curve of her ass taunting me from under the hem of her shorts.

"I'll have Rose send you out some food. You need something more than whatever is in the vending machines, and I know you're not going to go feed yourself properly." Tailen slung her leather bag around her front and it sat on her hip. She was right though, I was just going to go to the vending machines, the thought of something more substantial was enticing. So I wasn't going to argue with her.

"I'll make sure I don't fall asleep then." I stood up walking past her to grab the door, since her hands were occupied with the file box she had come with. She stopped in the doorway, a small smile on her face. " Is this going to be...."

"Awkward? Only if you make it that way Misha. I'm not done with you yet." Tailen leaned in planting a soft kiss on my cheek, lingering just long enough to make me let out a shuddering breath. I liked the way the last half of my nickname rolled off her tongue.

I watched as she got herself situated on that old tricycle, and rode away around the building. I shut and locked the door, before collapsing in the chair at the table.

If I thought yesterday was a lot, today had compounded on it. Four murders, suspect is a spirit that we have yet to identify, a woman who is almost too hot to handle, and my own memories that I kept in the depth of my mind creeping in to add just a bit more to the pile of stress. I held my head in my hands for a long while....just trying to figure out what to do next. Also while dealing with the ache in my groin that wouldn't seem to subside, I needed to eat and take a cold shower.

Thankfully I was able to get some sleep even if it was out of pure exhaustion. The couple of sandwiches, soup, and pastries Rose had one of her employees bring out to me last night was really what I needed. It came with a note that told me if she heard I wasn't eating again she would personally shove a donut where the sun doesn't shine. That woman was terrifying. After eating way more than I should have, I showered though it was mostly just me standing under the hot water and letting it run over me as I leaned against the glass wall, and then passed out on top of the covers of the bed.

I drove my way into town, parking in front of the police station. I decided that it was still too hot to put on my suit jacket, so I opted for a black t-shirt and work pants, my badge hanging from my belt, along with the holster for my firearm. As I entered the station, I tucked the arm of my sunglasses into the collar of my shirt. I was greeted by one of the only people I didn't want to see today.

Sheriff Southland was a tall man, slender, looked greasy due to him putting way too much product on his thinning black hair. His face was round, and he had a black mustache that he clearly used hair dye on to keep from turning grey. He spoke with the northern Michigan accent I had grown accustomed to since being here, though he spoke rather slowly and plodding like an old horse. He wasn't dressed in his normal uniform, and didn't seem to be on duty when I arrived, but nevertheless I had to act like I didn't want to toss him through a wall.

"Well well, see you got the Unknowns department involved in this one Agent Lewis, You think you got one of them critters committing the murders here in our town?" His tone made me want to hit him.

"I see that you got the faxes from the head office then." I kept my face neutral, and my tone even. Not wanting to get riled up like he wanted. "Could you get them for me please, along with the personal effects taken from the victims. They were not in the box of files you gave me." The man's face fell a little bit, as I wasn't taking his bait.

"Deputy, if you would get the Agent what he asked for, that would be a great kindness, thank you." One of the younger officers scurried off to the back offices to retrieve the items. "So are you going to tell me why you need them or are you going to just keep leaving me out of the loop."

"It's an ongoing investigation that was handed over to me, I prefer to do my own research before I ask for assistance, and considering it took me two days to get the coroners reports, I think I would work faster alone anyway."

"Now Agent, I don't know who you think your talking about, we do things the best we can around here. Sorry we don't move as fast as you city people." The Sheriff squared himself up to me on the other side of the desk. "If we got some creature roaming around our town killing people we ought to know about it."

"You will be the first to know when I find something worth telling."

"Maybe it is that woman, she could be one of those wendigos or vampires your little Unknowns division likes to investigate. From what I understand you only questioned her one time...maybe she pulled the wool over your eyes like she has with the rest of this..."

"You can leave Miss Galloway out of it, Sheriff. I already marked her off the list." I gritted my teeth, keeping my composure on the outside. He threw his hands up in front of himself, cocking his head to one side backing up a step.

"I'm just saying, something ain't right with that woman." The deputy came back at the right time with a new file box, it felt heavy as I yanked it away from him. A stack of copied papers stapled together on top of it.

"You have a good day, I'll give you any updates as I feel necessary." I spoke through gritted teeth.

I loudly pushed the station door open with my foot, and stomped back towards the SUV and threw the box on the passenger's seat. Rose had used the correct word. Blowhard. What was his obsession with her? Was he really stupid enough to think I would just arrest someone on his word? Fucking asshole.

I carefully moved through the mild mid-morning traffic of town, heading the couple miles out into the woods towards Tailen's cabin. It was actually nice to drive with the windows open, the fresh air filling my lungs, and the smells of the outdoors brought back happier memories of my childhood in northern California.

As I pulled in the gravel drive of the cabin, I heard the sound of music coming from the space under the house. Must be some kind of workshop, I could smell the scent of stale blood. Fuck. I could feel my heart rate spike, as I quickly jumped from the car.

I put my hand on my holster as I steadily approached. As I rounded the wall into the small workshop, I saw Tailen with a deer hide on her work bench, as she just finished rolling it up, and was rubbing salt over the roll of deer skin. The carcass of a deer hanging, draining in the far corner. Where on earth did she get a deer since last night?

"Well this is not what I was expecting to see first thing in the morning, though it's better than Sheriff Southland's ugly mug."

Tailen was dressed in a pair of very tight fitting spandex shorts, and a cut off white tank top that looked like it had been blood stained and washed many times. I had mixed feelings on if it was sexy or scary.

"Sal dropped her off this morning. I guess he got called to take care of it early this morning after a tourist hit her with their car. We always try to salvage what we can, respecting the animal. The meat may not be able to be used though, I'm pretty sure that it had some sort of illness. I figured I would get it skinned before Sal takes it back out to the woods to let it go back to the earth." The effortless way she spoke about the animal told me she had been doing this a long time, and genuinely cared for the animals that she and her friend hunted.

I knew very well what it took to process a deer. My father had taught my brother and I how to bow hunt at a fairly young age. I remember hating the process at first, but it got easier as each time we dressed a deer, he would explain how we were going to use it to feed ourselves, how we were to use as much as possible, and how to show respect by never killing more than we would need. It had been many years since I saw someone up close starting the tanning process.

The deer carcass in the corner did look a little strange. Not that it got hit by a car, strange either. The muscles of the animal looked a bit atrophied, and I noticed a protrusion on its hide quarters. Seemed likely that it would be a tumor of some sort. It was best to just let it go back to the earth then. I turned my attention back towards Tailen, she was pushing the hide down into a large bucket, and snapping the lid on easily.

"I must have lost track of time, we can head up, if you would like." Tailen was wiping off her hands and arms with a towel, though she still had a bit of blood splashed across her torso and the front of her legs. "Sal showed me how to use the coffee pots timer, so it should be finished brewing." She tossed the towel over her shoulder and headed up the stairs. I was not going to complain about being able to follow behind her.

The cabin's main room smelled like the amazing coffee she had on my first visit. I am pretty sure it's the same as the beans that Rose uses at her cafe. I would have to find out what they were so I could take them back home with me to Detroit.

"Go ahead and make yourself comfortable, I'm going to rinse off. I'm sure you can find creamer in the fridge." Tailen walked off towards the far end of the room past the couch and bed. I watched as she tapped the bathroom door shut with her foot, me catching the sight of her pulling off those skin tight shorts just before it latched closed.

I shook my head back to the task at hand: coffee making. I opened the smaller refrigerator, noticing there wasn't much in it. A few bundles of what I assumed to be deer meat, condiments and the carton of creamer. I made myself a nice cup of bean juice, and realized that I didn't know how she took her coffee. Pouring her a cup, I left it black and sat next to the pot. I figured it would cool down a little bit for her. I decided to take the time she was showering to be a bit nosey. Her home was decorated and filled with seemingly interesting things.

Sipping my cup, I followed the lines of the shelves, she had all sorts of things seated on them. Some handwritten books, some printed, jars of liquids and powders, skulls from small animals, and trinkets from different parts of the world. Everything had age to it. Nothing looked very new, but She seemed like someone who wasn't horribly interested in the modern day. Stopping at one shelf I pulled a book from it and set my coffee down, I opened it to can the pages. It had Farsi on the spine, and as I flipped through the pages, it had text written in the language As well as annotations on some of the drawings in German. I must have gotten lost in thought in the pages, because I felt a hand snake around my middle, and a chin rest on my shoulder, her wet hair tickled my ear.

"Ah, that's a good little book. Lots of information about occult practices of the region. A friend gave it to me." Tailen's weight felt good against my back. I was realizing over the last few days how much I missed being touched by another person. I hadn't had any sort of non-one-night-stand sort of contact with another person for well over a year now.

"I should have guessed you would have occultism books, spirits and all that...." I flipped through the book a bit more, eyeing a page in particular with a large ritual looking circle drawn on it with quite a few annotations in the German handwriting.

"Have you been to Germany? My friend who gave it to me was German, which is why the annotations are in her language." I shook my head and placed the book back on the shelf, and grabbed my coffee.

"No, but the Farsi I recognized from my time in the middle east. I was deployed there several years ago with my battalion." I moved her hand from my middle, turning around to look at her. I could feel the words in the pit of my stomach.

I wasn't keen on talking about my time there but the book flooded some memories back into the forefront of my brain.

"Why don't you go get the evidence box, and if you want to talk, your hands will have something to do." It was apparent she could see something in my face that I was trying to hide. I wasn't going to ask further questions about the book. I just nodded in agreement.

The more time I spent around her....the more I was intrigued by her.

Who was she?

Chapter 7

Tailen

Sal had dropped the deer off pretty early this morning. Not that I minded, sleep wasn't something that came easy. It had been hit pretty hard by a car, the people were okay, but the deer sure wasn't. I enjoyed the process of tanning, and normally Sal would stay and help butcher the meat, but we decided against it due to the tumors we found. It wasn't worth the risk of eating or giving it to friends without knowing what it was. However the best part about the whole process this morning was the shower after.

The scalding water washing away the grime, and even some of the stress from the last few weeks. I always found joy in the little things. I finished up quicker than I would have liked. Not wanting to leave Mikhail waiting for too long, I dried myself, and threw on a long t-shirt. Going out to join Mikhail in the main living area.

I watched him head down to his vehicle to retrieve the box we needed to continue our work on the case. He seemed to need to talk, all this talk of spirits seemed to have drummed up something for him. I cleared the kitchen table, and took a drink of the coffee that he had poured for me while I rifled through the cabinets for gloves, I rightly imagined he didn't have any.

Mikhail returned in short order, his face seemed a little more stern. Setting the mug of coffee down, I watched closely as he started to unpack the box. Placing the plastic bags full of the victim's personal effects down on the top of the red table. He didn't take the opportunity to start talking so I prodded.

"What was your battalion doing in Iraq?" I joined him at the table, pulling on some of the latex gloves and opening one of the bags. I started to pull the smaller evidence bags out, laying them out so they were easier to see. I heard him inhale and sigh deeply before he speaking.

"I was munitions, and where we were they were mostly trying to clear terrorist cells out of smaller villages. I know there was a larger conflict elsewhere, but that's not where we were, we were out in the middle of nowhere most of the time. At a forward operating base. We were a small compound, just enough structures to house us. We spent most of the time out in the field. You get to do more than your job description when in a place like we were. Spent a lot of time sitting in the back of a gun truck with the boxes of rockets and grenades." He took a long sip of his coffee, and put the cup down a bit too hard. It cracked the handle a little. "Shit. Sorry."

"It's fine, they are not important, they came with the cabin when I moved into it." I started to pick through the clothing that came out of Frank's bag, going through the pockets. Pulling out a wallet, a sobriety chip, some receipts, and also falling out of his pockets was some dirt and rocks. The same was in his boots. "How long were you over there?"

"I was there for about 8 months. I got sent home with some others after one of the missions went wrong. We lost some good people." Mikhail placed the broken cup in the sink before coming back to join me in rifling through the evidence bags. "I'm still not fully sure what happened in that town, but I do know that it almost cost me my leg." He was starting to look uncomfortable, and ran his hand down the side of his thigh, as if the memory of the injury hurt. Maybe it was too much right now. "All this spirit stuff has been bringing thoughts back up from then. It feels familiar. Especially seeing Mrs. Bea."

"I wondered if you encountered something while you were there. There are a lot of ruins in Iraq that are old, and possibly filled with old spirits." I stopped myself from expounding on that further, as he started to look visibly more irritated, trying to hide emotion behind his straight face and large serious eyebrows. So a subject change was in order. "Have you read through the paperwork that your office sent over?"

I heard Mikhail let out a little bit of a relieved sigh, and he shook his head. He held the thick stack of papers out to me. I snapped off the gloves I had put on and took the papers from him. He sat down hard in one of the kitchen chairs. I flipped through the first few pages. They started detailing more of the town's history than I had gleaned from the archives so far. Granted this town really seems to like to put that past behind them.

The town of *Bear Rest Hallow* wasn't always called that. Back before the mine collapse in the 1960's it was called *Neisbeth Lake* after one of the families that had founded the town. That name had come up a lot in the articles and ledgers, and I hadn't realized how much of an influence they had since most of the ledgers also named other rich families and companies that had mines in the area. Apparently they were one of the originals. Also they are the one outlined in the papers from the Unknowns Department responsible for the mine collapse, and blamed for the downturn of the town that followed. I recall seeing some accusations thrown around in some of the news articles I found in one of the archive binders.

The Unknowns Department had been sent, along with their counterparts from other government entities to do some 'damage control' as they called it. The mine collapse happened starting in one of the larger chambers, which caused structural instability that trapped and killed over 100 people. It not only affected the mines owned by Neisbeth's company, but others in the area as well. It created instability in the land. The fear was that because the land was so heavy with iron that spirits would get trapped and create a bigger problem. Which, according to the person writing this report, did happen. Screaming could be heard in the mines for months following the collapse. The people that did manage to dig their way out from some of the tunnels that were closer to the surface were traumatized, rightfully so. Those they could get to speak on the event, were cagey on details and only spoke of the darkness, smell of blood and screaming.

Though it seemed that they were able to place protections over the area with rituals to quiet the unrest of spiritual activity, but given the instability of the ground now, most of the mines had to shut. Not just due to spirit activity. It seems they didn't actually ever find the direct cause of the collapse, because they couldn't get to the epicenter. It was deemed an unresolved accident and the owners were issued massive fines. The bodies never recovered and the government decided to just condemn the area.

That explains the mass exodus in the following years, and why the town's residents do not speak of the past at all. It is why the guides keep people from the foot of the mountain on the north side of the lake. Nowadays you wouldn't be able to tell it was full of mining tunnels, from a distance it was covered in trees. Even I hadn't ventured up there often. Animals didn't seem to like the area either. Which is always a good indication to leave a place be and let it go back to nature.

"Mikhail, can you find the binder of news articles for me? I think I remember there being one about Walter Neisbeith. Seems he's the one to blame for the mine collapse. If the town blamed him for the downfall of the town...."

"It would make sense he would have reason to stick around and a chip on his shoulder." He grabbed the binder and started to flip through it. His face went back to its normal resting seriousness. It didn't take him long to find an article about his death. "Looks like a few months after the accident, he was found dead in his office. Shot several times, and apparently the police never arrested anyone in conjunction with his death."

Pushing the binder across to me, he tapped the rather short article. An article on the next page said he left behind a wife and a daughter. The wife committed suicide, but no mention of the daughter. The couple was buried in a local cemetery but no one bothered to give them a proper headstone. I felt for his wife Carol and daughter Liandra. They suffered because he was greedy and impetuous.

"This makes me wonder if the town or one of the other business owners turned on him and the police turned a blind eye because he was blamed for the tragedy."

"It's a good theory, but why now? You would have mentioned another spirit in that cemetery if you had seen one, and being so close to town more people would be dead if he was on a revenge fueled rampage." Mikhail was right. I had not seen him before, or not that I could recall.

"Sometimes spirits don't follow their bodies, most of the time they do, but if he was killed at his office, and enough blood was spilled....he may be there. If they didn't find him for days his spirit may have attached itself to something he felt strongly about or the literal blood soaked land." Mikhail looked at me quizzically, his eyebrow raised.

"Spirits can be attached to things other than their bodies?"

"It happens sometimes, not often, but a violent death, especially if someone feels wronged, it could happen. Still doesn't explain how the victims were found all over town."

I was annoyed now, my eyes scanning the table before us, with all the effects of the victims spread across it. A flash of orange peaking out from the corner of Franks wallet caught my eye.

"Mikhail, can you pull that orange paper out of that wallet?" Pulling a glove on he opened the wallet and set down the orange slip of paper. It was small, torn, and had just a phone number written on it. " I think I have seen this before."

Standing up, I went to where I had tossed my satchel the night before, in a heap on the bed, and dug around for a few moments. Grabbing the cluster of papers I had pulled off the community board from the library. There it was, the bright orange 'Now Hiring' paper, with tabs of phone numbers torn off the bottom of it. It had a phone number, 'cash paid daily', typed on it. Poorly made for sure, but nothing out of the ordinary.

Mikhail must have been thinking what I was, and I felt a twinge of excitement in my chest. A connection was being made.

Three other slips of paper of the same type were found in the pocket and wallet of two of the other victims.

"Tailen, this is an out of state number. Have you seen postings from them before around town?" I shook my head to the question, but it wasn't honestly uncommon for people to be looking for odd jobs in town to be done and post them in the paper or on the board. This one was just weird because of the number.

"Not uncommon to see postings no, do you want to call it? It's the connection at least linking three of them. Wonder why the police didn't catch this." I knew why. They thought it was me. I couldn't help but feel a little vindicated.

"Where is your...ah." His eyes scanned the room for my phone. It hung on the wall next to the door. Taking the paper with him he quietly dialed.

I was running through my brain for answers. Nothing was adding up currently, maybe they all had taken work and got ambushed by the angry spirit? But how did they get scattered around town? Was someone covering it up? The town had covered up things before, and having a bunch of men die on a job site as tourist season closed in, I wouldn't put it past anyone. Though I knew the police weren't in on it. Those idiots could barely make traffic stops.

I heard the phone click back on the hook. Mikhail looked a little pleased.

"It's a demolition company. I bet they bought some of the old mining properties to tear down for scrap. I should visit the auditor's office and see if they purchased any of the Neisbeith owned places…if we are making the correct assumptions, we may be able to find out who killed these men." He looked at the table and then walked past it, and me to my sofa. He sat down with a thud, and leaned back on it rubbing his face.

"It's a good thing right? A break in the case as they say." I followed him to the sofa, and sat down close to him.

"Well that's all I have. I'll be honest with you. If it is in fact the vengeful spirit of a dead mining baron…I'm not sure how to handle that. This is out of my department's reach, and very out of my knowledge."

"As long as we can prepare properly, I know how to deal with that. Problem is you explaining to your bureau why a strange woman who was on your suspect list was allowed at a crime scene." I thought that was funny, and even chuckled a bit. I leaned back on the sofa cushions looking at the ceiling. Putting my bare feet on the side of his leg. I felt his hand come down, and rest on my ankles.

"I don't think I will have a choice. I'm not stubborn enough to refuse the help of someone who clearly has a better grasp on the situation than I do."

"Then, I will do my best to prepare. There are a few ways to send spirits off, or help them rest. Hopefully we will be able to do it peacefully."

I didn't want to have to resort to violent means to get rid of a spirit. It could get messy, and worst of all Mikhail could get hurt if we didn't do something right. I had to prepare. I liked this man. It had been a while since I felt a connection like this with another, and it was something I wanted to hold on to.

I let myself be driven by emotion and heart sometimes. It has led me to some of the best connections. Rose, Sal, and Marcella for instance. Spending my time helping Mikhail was good. Though admittedly at first it was just for fun, to tease him, I found myself wanting to know more about him. Wrap my arms around him when I saw him struggling telling me just a snippet of his life from the military.

His pager started to vibrate at his hip. He pulled it from his belt and looked at the number.

"That would be Charlotte. I guess she is back from leave. I'll call her when I get back to the motel." I gave him an eyebrow raised look, he had yet to refer to someone back at the office by any name, let alone a first name.

"Who's Charlotte?"

Chapter 8

Mikhail

I realized from the very confused tone that Tailen had taken that I hadn't mentioned Charlotte before. It hadn't been needed, as she wasn't involved in the case, and I hadn't even thought I would hear from her while I was working on this one on my own. Well, not alone currently.

"She is my partner back at the bureau. Been out for almost a month taking care of her mother in Ohio." I felt Tailen's feet shift on my leg, pushing herself to sit 'properly' on the couch. "I hadn't thought to mention her, since she has been out of the office."

"That makes sense. Will they be sending her down to assist now that she is back in the office?"

"Not sure, I will have to call and see what she wants to do. Extra hands are always good though, since we only seem to have the one good lead." Was I detecting jealousy? She didn't seem the type. That couldn't be the case.

"I agree, fresh eyes would be good. Especially if the FBI lab found anything more than the county did on the particulates and labs." The tone I had detected faded as she spoke, and stood heading back to the table full of evidence. "I should help you clean this up."

"Are you upset with me?" I followed her and placed a hand on her shoulder.

"Not at all Mikhail, I'm just surprised you didn't tell me about her, it's an important person to leave out. It would be like me never mentioning Rose." She did have a point. I had worked with Charlotte for the last two years, and It is expected that more than one person would be sent on cases.

"You might be right, but like I said it didn't seem pertinent, and I have been tired." I squeezed her arm and started to help her pack the evidence bags away. The gloves she had were almost too small for my hands. If she was telling me the truth, it was interesting she was more irritated with me not mentioning someone I am close to.

"You should take the night to rest. Get some real sleep, get something good to eat. There isn't anything either of us can do tonight." She closed up the box tightly. The sound of the cardboard scraping somehow felt louder than it usually did and made me internally cringe.

She turned back to me, and smiled slightly. Her damp hair had flopped down to one side, covering up one of her eyes. I felt compelled to reach to her face and move it, pushing it back behind her ear. My mind was too full to do anything further than let my hand linger for a few moments. Tailen pushed her cheek into my hand and then stepped away. I nodded and took the box, once more heading back to my SUV.

"I will see you tomorrow Mikhail. Let me know what you find." She held the door for me, leaning on the railing of the stairs, watching me as left. I waved and pulled away down the road heading back into town. I was hungry, and I wasn't going to take her advice. I really wanted something greasy to eat. Well if I was honest with myself, I didn't want that either. I wanted to stay, and taste her again.

The discussion that had started about my time in the Army crept back into my head, as I ate my dinner, that was quickly obtained from a burger shack that was on the way back to my motel. I didn't think about it much, as it was fuzzy and incomplete in the back of my brain. I could remember bits and pieces of the encounter. I was in the back of a truck. I remember an explosion, screaming and falling off the back of the truck when it hit a large rock. The feeling of my leg being ripped up one side as I hung onto the bumper. The feeling of hot blood soaking my uniform, and a chill that permeated the air. The sound of the screams was piercing, I remember it hurting my ears.

I also remembered that when we were debriefed, we were told that we were involved in an IED explosion. I was never quite sure if they were telling the truth. They counted on the chaos to be unclear in our minds. The incident was the reason that many of us did not reenlist and went onto other things after the military. Though, with this case, I wasn't sure that it was much better to have joined the FBI. I didn't like the uncertainty it was making me feel. Humans killing people was easy to solve. This? This was different.

I swerved the car back into my lane as I heard the loud sound of a car horn. I must have lost myself for a moment in my thoughts. I needed to keep that in check while I was driving. Maybe I really did need more sleep, I needed something to organize my thoughts. A break from reading all those files would be good. I parked the car, and took the box of evidence into the room with me, groaning as I looked around the rather messy room. Maybe it wasn't just my brain that needed organizing. I was never good at keeping things in order.

I had a call to make. Back to the office, well to Charlotte who should still be in the office. I sat in the armchair by the bed and grabbed the whole telephone, dialing in the number that I knew by heart, and her extension.

"This is Agent Clark." A feminine voice, with exasperation in her voice answered the ringing phone.

"It's Agent Lewis, just returning your page. I didn't expect you to be back already." I leaned back, trying to relax into the slightly uncomfortable chair. Why did they even put these things in the rooms? Stupid cuck chair.

"Mikhail! I was wondering when you were going to call. I sent that page a couple hours ago. Mom is doing much better, so she basically told me to leave and go back to work because, and I quote 'your country needs you'. I didn't want to argue anymore with her."

"Have you seen the files that have been sent over yet, or just getting settled back in today."

"I got a small brief, what's all this about involving the Unknowns Department? This is a first for you, I know you think they are a bunch of quacks." She stifled a bit of a laugh as she spoke, which for some reason was irritating. Maybe it was the bright cheery tone of her voice.

"It's not easy to explain. Are they sending you down?"

"It hasn't been decided yet, but it would seem likely as this case seems to need more eyes on it. You have been up there since midweek and haven't sent much in the way of updates. You know how our director gets when there aren't daily updates."

"I'm fully aware that he sits in his office and pretends to work, if he does send you down, I will be able to explain better. Just let me know, and do me a favor, get those guys down in Unknowns a box of bagels from that place on First Street."

"I can do that. Hopefully I will see you soon." I heard the phone click, and I sunk back into the chair more.

One more person to keep track of, at least she was a good agent, and a smart one. It wouldn't be a hindrance to have her hands in the mix.

Why did the summer have to be so hot? It was another day where my suit jacket would continue to live on the back of the chair in my motel room. Though I decided that a button down was more appropriate than a t-shirt for visiting the auditor's office today.

It was located inside of the courthouse building in the center of town. The office was on the second floor and there was a middle aged man sitting behind a desk typing away on a computer. He looked a little frazzled and didn't seem to notice me coming in through the creaky old door.

"Excuse me. Are you who I need to talk to about property information?" I made sure that my tone was serious, professional. Though it still seemed to startle the man away from his work.

"Who? What?" He cleared his throat and looked up at me from behind the computer screen. "Oh, yes, how can I help you?" I saw his eyes glance down at the badge on my belt.

"I need to know if *Old World Demolition* has bought any property in the town over the last few months. It pertains to the ongoing investigation I am working on." I let my hands rest with my thumbs in my belt.

"Actually, I haven't gotten around to putting that paperwork into the computer yet, short staffed since it's summer you know." He pushed back away from his desk and back towards an inbox basket. I watched as he thumbed through the paperwork. "This about those four murders? I don't see why a bunch of old properties would have anything to do with all that."

"I'm not at liberty to discuss the ongoing investigation, but I assure you I wouldn't be taking you from your work if it wasn't important."

The man nodded and mumbled about needing more help in the office, finally producing some papers that were stapled together. He handed them over, and checked the stack again.

"Those are copies, so feel free to take them with you. Let me know if I can help you with anything else." He almost immediately went back to his computer. He liked his work I guess. I nodded in thanks and let the man go back to his typing.

I leaned on the wall out in the hallway, opening up the documents and giving them a quick go over. The company had bought a few different buildings but one stood out to me as the name was shared with our spectral suspect: The Neisbieth mining offices and smelting factory. They were purchased for very cheap about two months ago and it had permits for demolition. Probably going to knock them down and scrap what they could, no other permits for building or rezoning were in the packet. Which was odd; there wouldn't be enough money in just scrapping and demoing old build-ings, without wanting to put something else on the site. The intention may be to just apply for the permits later, closer to when they wanted to build. Either way, we had a place to check out. I needed to grab that old map from the motel room if I wanted to actually figure out where it was located. First though, coffee.

I tucked the folded papers under one arm heading out into the town center. Why did it seem hotter here than in the city? The town bustling had died down a bit since it was the start of the week, people heading back to their homes from their weekend of playing in the woods. *Rose's Café* was even a little dead. Though it was in the lull between breakfast and lunch. I could see a few tables with people, but nothing like it had been over the long weekend. I did notice the now familiar old trike sitting against the wall.

I'm not sure I had heard Tailen properly laugh in the days I had known her. It was higher pitched than I would have thought, a small snort escaping which made Rose laugh even harder. What an odd pair the two of them were. A woman with black hair, dressed in black slightly tattered shorts and t-shirts with heavy looking boots, and the other dressed in a pristine pink and white waitress dress with pulled back blonde hair with high heels. They both looked at me as I walked in, Tailen spinning on the counter's stool to greet me.

"Good Morning Sugar!" Rose's exuberance was almost too much before coffee, but she poured me some in short order as I took a seat next to Tailen at the counter. I would enjoy the heat of the mug more if it wasn't so hot outside. I felt Tailen run her booted foot up the side of my leg.

"Did you manage to find anything over at the auditor's office?" Tailen looked down in her coffee mug, staring at the black liquid.

"I got paperwork, yes. Turns out they bought up some of the old derelict buildings that the mining companies owned, including one that Niesbeith owned. Just need to figure out where it is, so I can go check it out."

"You mean we, I'm not letting you go out to a building alone that has a potential killer spirit roaming around." I had to agree with a nod, she wasn't wrong. If I did that I might end up like the other four.

"Did you say Niesbeith Darlin? That fool's old factory is up on the eastside of the lake. Not easy to get to though, they let the roads go to shit a long time ago." Rose set her coffee pot down fairly hard on the counter, cocking her eyebrow at me and Tailen. "Why would you need to go up there? Isn't nothing but dust and pain up there."

"I told you Rose, I think that Niesbieth man's spirit may be the reason for all this."

"You may have mentioned it, but I didn't know he was going to drag you out to that dump." Rose seemed a lot more agitated about us going there than she should be.

"How do you know where the place is?" I asked before sipping my coffee, making eye contact with her, though the perfection of her face unsettled me. She just pursed her lips slightly giving a harumph noise.

"She grew up here Mikhail." Said so simply, like I should have known that the gorgeous Barbie behind the counter grew up in a podunk old mining town.

"Half right, we got here around the time when people were leaving. Parents said property would be cheap." Rose inter-jected.

That's when I heard the door of the cafe swing open, and one of the last people I wanted to see made his way in. His voice grated on my last nerve.

"Well well Agent Lewis, I see you are making cozy with a murder suspect, I guess this is why you about bit my head off yesterday at the office." Sheriff Southland's cocky attitude spilled out of his mouth, and I about had it.

"Sheriff Southland, I told you. She has been struck from the suspect list, there isn't any evidence to accuse Miss Galloway of these murders. You need to know when to quit with your dramatics." I spun around on the stool, standing up. He was taller than me, but by no means more intimidating.

"I'm just saying, I understand. These women got you wrapped around their little fingers, so you don't suspect her. Don't think I haven't got eyes all over this town seeing you leaving the library after her, heading out to her cabin. I'm not the one getting played by a murderer."

"You need to kindly....step the fuck off Sheriff. You are out of line." I could feel my blood boiling under my skin. I took a step towards him.

"I don't think I am Agent. You come out here thinking you know better than my department, we could have handled this, It was the mayor who made me call you. Maybe I should call your boss, let him know about this...."

The shattering sound of the coffee pot smashing to the tile floor quieted the whole place. I heard the sound of Rose's heels stomp loudly as she came around the counter, and I swore her eyes were red.

"If you ever want to eat in this restaurant again Morgan Southland you will shut your goddamn mouth. How fucking dare you come into my business...into my house and spew your nonsense for everyone to hear." She had pushed between us at this point. She was nose to nose with him, and I have never seen a man back down that quickly. "I heard enough of your ramblings for weeks, I let it go. NO FUCKING LONGER. GET THE FUCK OUT. NOW."

The sheriff backed off a step and made a disgusted face, though I could tell there was fear behind his eyes. He wagged his finger at me in warning and shot Tailen a look of hatred before he took off back across the street to the station.

I watched as Rose patted her hair back into place, and smoothed the apron on the front of her before turning back, her face was flushed but she was back to her normal smiling self. One of her staff was already cleaning the broken glass from the floor. She sat herself in the stool that I had inhabited. Her arms grabbed Tailen, who mildly resisted the embrace.

"I'm sorry, I just couldn't take it anymore. All you are doing is trying to find the killer before someone else gets hurt, and that child of a law man can't keep his panties out of a bunch long enough to let you do your job."

"I won't lie....that was very impressive. I don't think I could have put him in his place better." I was, in fact, impressed.

Though it reinforced my notion that Rose was not a force to be trifled with. Tailen, however, seemed a bit unbothered, used to the Sheriff popping off at her in such a way.

"Thank you friend." Was all she managed to get out. Rose squeezed her and righting herself, went back behind the counter to ready some to go coffee. It was weird how she always seemed to know exactly when I was leaving.

"Tailen, why don't we go get the map, and we can see about checking the place out, there should be enough daylight. I don't exactly want to get caught out there once the sun is down." She nodded, quietly sliding off her stool, giving Rose a kiss on the cheek as she handed the coffees to her.

"Here." She handed me mine as we stepped onto the side-walk outside of the cafe. "You should go get the map, and then meet me at Sal's. I think if we are going up to the eastside of the lake, we should have him take us in the truck. Your SUV isn't made for the rough terrain."

I couldn't fault her logic on that. Plus, If they hunted these woods, he may know his way around better.

"At his garage then?"

"That's the place." She shifted on her feet slightly and looked over at the police station.

"That man will get what's coming to him one day if Rose has her way. It doesn't bother me the things he says, or the insults he has hurled my way even before this. I'm sorry you had to listen to his vitriol."

"He shouldn't be in his position if he's going to cause scenes like that, and not you or Rose, or anyone should have to put up with that bullshit he spews."

We parted ways though I lingered to watch her on the trike heading to meet with Sal. Once she was out of sight I hopped into my SUV and headed to grab the map.

It was only noon and the day already felt long.

Chapter 9

Tailen

The Sheriff's outburst at the cafe was not horribly surprising, he had many times tried to rile me up. I expect it was because he wanted me to attack him, or give him reason to toss me in jail. I had dealt with worse than him in my life. There were far scarier things in this world than a man who had too much power and not enough sense. The funniest part was he thought he could do it in Rose's cafe. That's the last bridge anyone in town would want to burn.

We were getting close to answers, which was a satisfying feeling. It had been a long time since I had tasked myself with anything other than just living day to day. I had allowed myself time to enjoy the small things, to rest, to make friends in this small town that I had moved to. Though the itch to do something beyond that had been creeping in, which was being scratched by this case. What an odd feeling.

Sal was sitting on the tailgate of his truck when I pulled up to the garage. I always enjoy the sight of his smiling face, which currently has a large black hand print on it.

"You know, I think the grease is supposed to stay in the cars." I laughed and gestured to his face. He shrugged as he jumped off the tailgate rubbing his face with a rag retrieved from his back pocket.

"Considering that car drove out of here just fine, I'm sure it could spare some of its grease." He embraced me as he always does, the tightness of his arms always seemed to soothe any of my mind's problems, even if just for the moment.

"I need your help Sal." He let me go and smoothed his mustache with his fingers.

"Anything you need. Related to the case I'm guessing? Marcella said you borrowed a bunch of old books from the archives." He gestured for me to follow him into the garage. I loved the smell of this place. The air was fragrant with the smell of oil, gasoline, and the kerosene from a currently unused heater. I tucked my trike just inside the door.

"It is, and we need a ride. Also, if you happen to have some salt and deer blood for a spirit binding ritual, and possibly a shotgun." I leaned on the old Mustang currently sitting in the garage bay.

"So we were right? I'm really happy to help now." Sal got that look on his face like he always did before a hunt. Satisfaction. "We need salt, shells, and animal blood, and..." He kept muttering as he walked hurriedly over to the other side of the garage.

He was right. The ritual called for blood. Deer would work which I knew he had in abundance from our hunts. I wanted to bind the spirit back to its body. Then it couldn't hurt anyone any longer. It was the least messy way to deal with it. At least I hoped it would. It had been a long time since I had to delve into that sort of knowledge, and certainly not since being here as the iron in the ground of this town did a good job of keeping the spirits in their graves. Though they were trapped and couldn't move on, as most people put it.

I reached into my bag at my hip, and pulled out a small black book. Opening it to gaze at its pages. It was the place I had written down important rituals and spells, compiled from other books in my collection. The memories of the paper flooded into my mind, I could recall most of the words, written in an array of languages from the countries of origin. The pages were soft and worn, they felt like silk under my finger tips. I closed the book as I saw Sal returning with his haul of items. He set them down on the workbench. Joining him at his side, he motioned for me to help him pack the jars, and small boxes into a larger duffle bag. The shot gun was broken open, he went about checking its mechanics and making sure the firing mechanism worked. It was a fine double barreled shotgun, old and well used with a wooden stock.

"It's been a long time since this old girl has been used, but she should do the trick. I have the sneaking suspicion you're going to hand it over to that Agent." Sal side eyed me and

I nodded. He wasn't wrong. I wasn't going to ask Sal to actually engage with a spirit if we did find one. I wasn't going to risk my friend or Marcella's wrath for getting her fiance hurt.

"I was hoping you wouldn't complain about it too much."

"I'll be fine. Glorified chauffeur then. I don't think I could handle facing Frank's potential killer anyway."

I heard the sound of tires crunching on the gravel outside of the garage and the slam of Mikhail's heavy SUV door closing and locking. I tightened my satchel a little and grabbed the duffle bag to head out to the truck. Mikhail was back lit by the afternoon sun in the garage door.

"Been packing?" He took off his sunglasses and placed them in the collar of his shirt. I really did like the way his chest hair looked in that shirt. I shrugged the bag higher on my shoulder.

"Salt and iron shells, blood ...the usual things. Sal has something with a little more kick than that thing." I gestured to his hip, he gave me a slightly disgruntled look as if I had insulted him, and not the standard issue pistol hanging from his belt.

"I didn't know I would need something with more kick." Sal approached and roughly handed him the shotgun.

"Well the shells are easier to pack for this old thing than it is for that. Tailen's right too, if you are dealing with a specter, you're gonna need something that can deal with it. Regular bullets won't do the trick. Now if you excuse me, I need to freshen up a bit before we head out. Y'all figure out where we are headed." The sound of the coverall zipper being pulled down made me laugh a little as Sal made his way towards the garage's office. How he never got his chest hair caught in the zipper of his coveralls I will never know.

I tossed the duffle into the bed of the small truck, and hopped up on the tailgate plopping down with my legs hanging off the edge, feet dangling.

"Mikhail, did you look at the map yet?" He nodded his head, plucking the roll out of the back of his pants, and set it down next to me. Though he seemed more interested in the shotgun he had been handed.

"I haven't. I also haven't used a gun like this since I was a teenager. Not as sophisticated as the newer ones they issue now." He turned it over in his hands. Men always seemed to like guns, they were weapons of destruction. Useful, helpful even sometimes, but I wasn't keen on using them myself.

I opened up the map, noting where we were going was about ten miles east of the lake, which was now mostly wooded, but there was probably still a dirt or gravel road that was used for access. If it had been used recently we would be able to tell. I turned the map around and pointed at it. Things up in that area were a bit spread out, as it used to be deforested due to the traffic that would have been in the area hauling raw iron in, and processed out.

"It's not exactly close, but it shouldn't take too long to get out there unless there are a lot of trees blocking our way. It used to be a pretty well used road, but now a days, it's all woods."

"I can see why you would want to take a smaller truck then. Mines not made for off roading, considering it barely fits in the city streets." He slid the shotgun up into the back of the truck next to the duffle. I studied the map again for a few moments, until I felt his hand slide up my leg.

"It's a wonder they let big things like that on city streets that were not built for them." I folded the map back. Looking down at his hand, it felt nice to be touched by him. I turned my gaze up. He had a small look of concern on his face, I could tell he was feeling uneasy.

"If you are feeling unsure, we can give it a day. Give it more planning time, just in case." I rested my hand on his arm. I felt him squeeze my thigh slightly.

"It's not that. I'm just.." He looked away from me and towards the sky. "There are a lot of things I don't understand, and this case has been unprecedented for me. If I didn't have a feeling of uneasiness I would think I finally lost it." For some reason this made me laugh. It seems that he was more easily sharing his thoughts today.

"It will be fine, we will be as prepared as we can be." I decided boldness was in my blood today. "And when it's over, we can finish what you started the other day when you were so very tired." His eyes snapped back to mine, his serious face in its usual state.

"That I started? I started that. Yes, it was me. Not you pushing my buttons." He pressed closer to me, resting against the tailgate. I could have wrapped my legs around him.

"I am more than happy to push more of them." I leaned my face close to his, "After we take care of this investigation. I really want to get that shirt back off you."

"You know, if you guys need to take a cold shower before we head out there is one in the office." Sal had apparently snuck up on us while I was distracted. Mikhail pulled away faster than I would have liked, and though he held that serious look on his face, it was blushed pink.

"I think we will be alright, Sal. Whenever you are ready." I pushed myself up into the bed of the truck all the way, and Sal closed the tailgate. I handed the map back to Mikhail. " Just show it to him, he should know the way mostly but you're on navigation." I found a good spot against the cab of the truck, crossing my legs , and a good place to hold on should I need to.

The sound of the doors slamming shut and the engine roaring to life meant we were on our way. Heading back though town towards the lake that was central to the life of this place. Even though the lake was where almost everyone who came to town was interested in staying, everything was concentrated on the south and west sides of it. The guides wouldn't really take people to other places. Too dangerous with all the old mines, and buildings left over from the town's old days. Plus, it lets them maintain the town's image without much thought. Besides, if you got too far up into those parts of the woods, animals ceased to be heard and it made the quietness almost too much. Tourists were happy to jet ski, boat, and swim closer to the south shore because it was the most convenient.

I, myself, had only ventured with Sal once or twice up to the north shore of the lake, but it was in pursuit of deer during one of our hunting nights. Even then it made Sal uneasy, I wouldn't say that I was a fan of it, and until this case came along, I wasn't interested in chasing the uneasy feeling like I would have earlier in life.

The feeling of the truck changed as it bumped off the well traveled pavement and onto gravel. We had entered the road that went around the lake. I took the opportunity to push up and look out the side of the truck bed. The sun beaming down on my face felt nice. As we traveled down the road, slower than on the pavement I took the moment to enjoy the heat that seemed to bother Mikhail so much.

I could see the two men chatting through the window in the back of the cab. It was muffled and I only hoped that Sal wasn't drilling Mikhail on our interaction on the tailgate. Though it would be rather amusing. Mikhail, though a little stoic couldn't seem to hide it when he was embarrassed, the color of his face always betrayed him.

It was a little while before I felt the truck turn onto softer ground, slowing even further as the trees and forest debris closed in a little closer to the truck. I had to catch myself a few times on the side of the truck bed after going over substantial bumps. Maybe I should have worn longer pants. The tree coverage grew a little heavier. It was getting quieter, no longer being able to hear the sounds coming from the lake as we moved further from it's shores.

Just as I was feeling lost in my own thoughts, I heard a knock at the back window, I looked up to see Mikhail gesturing forward. Grabbing the side of the truck, I pulled myself up, leaning my weight on the truck cab so I could look over the top of it. I ducked my head to avoid a low hanging branch, and the truck crept up the path. I could tell by some broken branches, another vehicle had been through here. Though how long ago, I didn't know. I could see old dilapidated fencing coming into view, as well as the crumbling walls of old guard shacks. We had arrived.

The old factory was in ruins. It was grown over with vining plants and brush, but the walls of the main buildings were still standing, even if they were worn and full of holes with limited vegetation growing from them. There were several buildings, large trucks turned over on their sides from breaking down, and piles of unrefined iron around the property. I felt the truck stop in what would have been the center hub of the property. Scanning the area I could see fresh-ish tire tracks. So someone had been out here. Which meant we were on the right track, That made me feel a bit relieved.

"This seems like the place Tailen." Sal said as he jumped out of the cab of the truck and came around to the side looking up at me. "It's quiet, I don't like that." I saw his nose crunch up a little bit and he crossed his arms. "What's the plan?"

"I will need you out here Sal, just in case." I tossed him out the duffle bag and grabbed the shotgun. I swung my legs over the side of the truck as Mikhail came around the side, I slid to the ground and handed him the gun. "I think we should check out the offices, that's where Niesbeth was found. So we should go there first, but I'm not sure what building though."

I walked in front of the truck and let my eyes travel between the buildings. One was clearly the factory where the smelting happened, as it still had one of the smoke stacks crumbling out of its roof. It surprised me that the buildings were made of brick, considering most things in this town were predominantly made with iron. There was a building connected to it by a walkway on the second story. Though the walkway was half fallen, it was mostly intact.

"We should head in there." I heard the sound of shells sliding in the shotgun and it closing with a heavy click. " Mikhail pointed to the building that was connected to the factory, it made sense. It was the plainest of the buildings, minus the falling sign over the large double doors that had the first half of the name Neisbeth hanging on by barely a screw.

"I'll be here Tailen, just yell if you need me. I'll keep my eye out for anything weird." I patted Sal on his shoulder before taking the duffle from him, and it was promptly taken from me by Mikhail and thrown over his shoulder and across his chest.

The large buildings loomed over us as we approached, I could feel something in my chest. A pressure. Bad things happened in this place, and I don't think it was just one death. If the industrial revolution taught us anything it was that places like this were built on the backs and blood of the common man. It was an uneasy feeling as the double doors creaked open and we entered the dusty foyer of the old building.

The light coming through the holes in the walls and roof made the dust swirling around in the air almost beautiful. If we weren't here trying to find a murderous spirit, I would be inclined to stay and take it in.

But we had work to do.

Chapter 10

Mikhail

The ride out was bumpier than I had hoped, I wasn't used to the pseudo off roading we were doing in the old truck. I had the grab the handle above the door a few more times than I would have liked. Although I would take it over the probing that Sal did during the ride.

"Getting a bit close to Tailen, eh? I guess that means you don't share the Sheriffs notions of her murdering nature?" Sal didn't take his eyes off the dirt 'road' as he spoke.

"She was taken off the list after I met with her the day I arrived." I was not trying to talk about my feelings with someone I had barely even spoken to. Though he seemed to be close to her.

"Ah, avoiding it. Alright. I mean she is quite the person isn't she. I'm sure you have noticed that she isn't much like the rest of the people in town."

"She is interesting, not what I would have thought when I walked into her cabin. I assume she isn't from around here."

I gripped the handle again as we hit a huge bump. That one made my ass hurt. What were these seats made out of?

"Tailen is from lots of places. Not here, though. I for one am glad to have her here. Good friends are hard to come by Agent Lewis. Got to keep them close." I nodded in agreement, hoping he would stop, I was trying to keep my mind off of that sort of thing. Keep my head in the objective. Sal had one last thing to say before we saw the factory ruins come into view. "Just make sure if you want to be close to her, you accept that she isn't like you."

I didn't have a chance to ask what he meant as he was already jumping out of the truck. We had arrived.

The buildings were crumbling. No wonder people stayed away, it looked dangerous, and felt strange. It was all too quiet, no sounds of animals. The wind was almost too calm in this complex. The buildings shielded the area a bit from the sun, but it was still hot.

I followed Tailen with the shotgun slung on my shoulder, and duffle in hand as we headed towards the building that we determined to be the offices. I sometimes wondered why she always wore shorts. Maybe it was to torture me specifically.

"This place is just crumbling Tailen, keep your footing in here. I don't want to have to pull you out of a hole in the floor." My eyes traveled up from the dilapidated reception area, to the second floor. "I expect if he was the owner his office would be up there." I looked over to her, and she had pulled out a jar and popped it open. Salt. She stopped briefly in the center of the room, pouring a large circle around herself and then capping the jar again.

"If needed, this is a place we can retreat to. Salt is a bit caustic to Spirits."

"That explains the shotgun shells." I guess I always thought that salt was just an old wives tale, but I was being proved wrong again. I strode past Tailen, and checked the first few steps of the metal staircase heading up to the floor above. Rusted, but seemed solid enough.

"Someone has been here before us. I saw the tire tracks outside, I would expect the floors to be at least mostly solid." She spoke with confidence, and I couldn't disagree. So I headed up the stairs, they groaned the whole way up under our combined weight. She was behind me closely, both of our heads were on a swivel. In the back of my head I wish I had sent her up the stairs first, but this was not the time for that sort of thinking.

Papers littered the floor of the second story, along with broken desks and filing cabinets. The place had clearly been gone through many times over the years. There was a bit of graffiti on the walls, but it was very old and peeling off just like the rest of the paint on the walls. The name plaques on the offices had mostly fallen off the walls, but I saw Tailen bend down to pick one up. She held it up for me to read.

"Walter Neisbeth. Looks like we found the right place." She tossed the plaque back to the ground, stirring up the dust even further. "Let's see if he's home."

The air felt stale and warm, so if there was a spirit here it wasn't showing itself currently. Tailen pushed open the wooden door to the large office. It was pretty open, with a large wooden desk at one end, and cabinets lining one whole wall. The shelves were broken and falling out, ledgers and files scattered on the floor.

"A person has been here Mikhail, look." I walked around the large wooden desk to meet Tailen, there was a huge set of blueprints rolled out in the desk, but it looked like some pages were missing. Pieces of the torn pages still left in the staples.

"How do we know this was recent?"

"No dust." She ran her hand across the top page, and she was right. No dust had settled on them like they had on all other surfaces, and it now brought my attention to the fact that there were disturbed filing cabinets.

"That demolition company must have been up here, but what would they want with blue prints?" I walked to the file cabinets and tried to jerk open the drawer with my free hand. It just rattled the metal. Tailen continued to rifle around the desk, pulling open the top drawer. I watched as she gave the drawer a quzzical look. Then bent down putting her head under the drawer and dislodging something. She popped back up with a leather bound book in her hand. Well, a hidden compartment wasn't something I would have caught.

"I don't think that the article was correct about where Walter was killed. This desk is not blood stained in the slightest, the wooden floors are a consistent color." She was right, even after all this time, 50ish years on the wood would still be stained darker. The place was closed down right after his murder and besides moving the body, the clean up would have been minimal. "This is a diary…" She flipped through the old pages, I could see a bit of dust coming from the pages as she turned them. Tailen closed it and shoved it down into her satchel at her hip.

"I think you're right. What do you think someone would want those blueprints for…."

"There may be copies in the archives at the library, I'm not sure if permits would have been needed back then. All that's here is mine shaft blueprints, which is what I would expect."

I smacked the front of the filing cabinet in frustration. All this was telling us is that someone was here. There was no fresh blood, there was no evidence of a struggle. What were we missing? If anything, Tailen came up behind me and touched my back.

"We should check the factory floor. He was killed here, it wouldn't make sense for it all to be a lie. Let's move on." I couldn't argue with her logic. If he continued to run the place after the mine collapse, maybe it was the workers who finally turned on him.

Heading back to the main hallway of the second floor. We made our way carefully past other decaying offices. The unease of this place grew for me. I didn't like it. Turning around the corner at the end of the corridor, I could see where some of the floor had fallen out, into what looked like a kitchen below. However the door to the walkway between the two buildings was hanging by rusted hinges, and accessible. Against my better judgment I pulled it open, and it fell to one side hanging from its top hinge only. It made a horrible crunching noise. The sound grated on my ears and made me wince.

"I think the walkway is solid enough, watch your step Tailen." I went first onto the metal covered walkway. Some of the roof had fallen down onto the walk, but was easy to get over. Tailen yelled out to Sal, who acknowledged her with a wave and thumbs up. The afternoon sun actually made the plaza in front of the buildings look beautiful in a way. I could imagine that back in the day the plaza would have been bustling with activity on a day like today. Now, however, it was quiet.

I tugged at the door to the other building, it didn't budge. It just rattled a bit with my pull. Tailen came to my side, and wrapped her hand around the handle above mine. Taking her lead we both pulled the door almost flew off its hinges towards us. Tailen stopped it from hitting us with her free hand. I'm beginning to think she is stronger than she lets on, for having a smaller frame. I helped her push the door to the side, and had to re-situate the shotgun back into my hand. The smell of fire, soot, and metal hit me right in the face. It was weirdly strong considering the amount of holes in the sides of the building.

We entered the large expansive room on a metal walkway that used to go further up into a grid above the foundry floor. Now the only safe way it seemed to traverse was down some fairly sketchy looking stairs. Tailen seemed lost in her thoughts as she idly ran her hand over the railing. I allowed her to go first down the stairs, they creaked loudly under the weight of her heavy steps. The last one crumbled as she stepped on it, causing her to stumble forward a bit and she had to catch herself on a table.

"Are you okay?" I jumped down the last few steps, not wanting to test them.

"I'm fine, I should have expected it, the whole place is crumbling." Her tone was serious. I hadn't heard her like this yet, and it was incredibly unnerving considering she was flirty and full of wit usually. Something must be bothering her about this place as it did me.

The foundry floor was massive, containing the ruins of furnaces, the large vats that would have held molten iron were dropped to the floor from their mounts on the ceiling, save for one that I would not be going near. As it hung from basically a thread towards the far side of the building. Old conveyor belts were turned over and pushed towards the walls. Piles of unsmelted iron were in heaps around the furnaces that were now stopped up with what was once liquid metal. This place would have once been full of people, bustling in bad working conditions to smelt down the ore dug up in the mountain's mines. Now it was a derelict skeleton of a greedy business man's hubris.

Tailen had moved towards the central hub of the room. She stopped short, and looked down at her feet.

"It happened here....." She breathed In deeply, her eyes focusing on a huge stain in the concrete under her feet. The dark stained floor stood out from the discoloration of the concrete and one could almost see the outline of where the blood had pooled. "I'm going to start putting down the sigil." She motioned towards the duffle bag.

"What is it you are doing exactly? Is...is this even the place?" I handed the bag over, and Tailen quickly went to work unpacking a few jars of blood and salt.

"I'm going to draw a sigil, and use it to more or less trap the spirit. Hopefully bind it so it can't hurt anyone. A bound spirit could theoretically be returned to its body. Which could then be burned or covered in salt to keep it contained. Usually It would dissipate after a while, but in this town, that doesn't happen easily. I need you to keep watch. If the spirit manifests. Shoot it."

Her instructions were easy enough to follow. Her tone remained to the point. Which made me nervous. I wasn't used to the seriousness. I kept my eyes up and walked around the space she had chosen to draw. She cleared debris on the floor, giving herself some space. Then I smelled the blood. Stale animal blood. I glanced over to her on occasion. Her hand covered in blood, and she was muttering as she drew symbols on the floor. Crawling on all fours as she moved around in a circle, redipping her hand in the jar of blood as she needed. I didn't know that it would be so messy. It did make we wonder where the hell she learned to do this, and possibly why I was so trusting of a woman smeaing blood on the floor.

"Rituals require sacrifice. Depending on the incantation and sigil animal blood is suitable." sitting back on her feet and pushing up to standing she looked down at her work.

I could feel the air growing cold. Tailen looked up eyes going wide. Our breath was already becoming visible in the air. That's when I heard the creaking of the metal around us, as

if someone was walking on the catwalks above us. I raised
the shot gun upwards following the sound with the barrel
across the ceiling.

Tailen worked faster getting the salt out, hurriedly putting
an unbroken circle around the sigil. The air started growing
colder, and the hair on my arms started to stand on end.

The specter that started to form as it came down the dilapidated stairs was that of a heavyset tall man. Unlike Mrs. Bea
from the library, I could clearly see his features, he didn't
seem like he was floating. Although I could see through him,
he was like a projection. His face twisted up in anger. He
started to lunge from the stairs towards us and I fired off
the shotgun, sending salt and iron spraying the spector and
the area behind him. The man dissipated into nothing, but
the cold did not seem to stop.

Tailen pulled me roughly backwards into the circle of salt.
Her eyes were narrowed and she didn't speak. I got my
footing back under me, and listened. I could hear the sound
of heavy footsteps, this time on concrete. I swung around,
Tailen ducking out of the way. I could see the spirit forming
again, and I fired off another shot.

Tailen went to her knees, her hands placed on edge of the
sigil. I reloaded the shotgun from the shells I tucked in my
pocket.

"Mikhail, when I give you the signal, break the salt line."

"That doesn't seem like a good idea..." I could feel the tension of the room rising, and it was then I heard the large garage door at the front being pounded on and the muffled yell of Sal.

"He is only going to get more hostile. If I can get him in the circle. I can finish this." I had to trust her. I nodded in agreement.

The sounds around us were growing. Chains rattled, the metal of the catwalks rattled unnervingly above us. I was just waiting for it to fall. I had to trust that she knew what she was doing, I had no other option.

My hairs stood on end, he was coming again, and I could feel the rush of air as he manifested from near one of the downed vats. He was moving quicker this time. I found it hard to keep the shotgun trained on him. I felt the chill get closer and then Tailen's voice was shouting. I pushed my foot back, scattering the salt line, as the spirit slammed into the sigil.

Tailen panted as she stood up. It was like the spectral human was trapped in an aquarium. He thrashed around hitting the edges only to bounce back. It distorted his features as he did. His visage twisted in anger as he pounded against the invisible barrier. Tailen walked around the circle, her eyes trained on him. Only looking at me once she seemed satisfied.

"Good work." She reached into her bag, and pulled out a small black book, flipped a couple of pages.

I couldn't understand the words coming out of her mouth, and the inside of the circle looked like chaos. Then....the screaming. It was ear shattering, I took one hand off my gun to cover the side of my head. Clamping my eyes shut and tilting my head down. It reminded me of the sound an incoming mortar made.

The walls felt like they were shaking. The sound of cables snapping caught my attention. I looked up just as a piece of that overhead walkway came careening down from the ceiling. I felt a pair of hands on my chest as I was sent flying back from the impact zone. The slab of metal landing on the specter and Tailen. I could see her legs protruding from under the metallic floor.

"Fuck...Fuck." My head hurt, but I tried to stand. Where was the shotgun? My eyes adjusted from the impact. All I could see was the spirits hands reaching for me. I screamed as his hand gripped my shoulder picking me up. His distorted face was too close to mine.

The chaos seemed to slow down as I dropped back to the floor. There was a blackness curling around the spirit, which is why he seemed to let me go. Dark tendrils gripping him, the distortion on his face went from anger to pain. The screaming began again, but it was anguish. I couldn't even get anything to come out of my throat. The pain of my shoulder and the creeping of the chill that was setting into my chest.

I watched as the specter was ripped in twain in front of me. It wasn't like when I hit him with the shotgun blast. This was different, like he had been ripped from reality. His spectral form melding into the blackness of the tendrils before they started to pull back to their point of origin. The figure backlit by the afternoon sun, long black hair, smokey shadowed tentacles undulating behind as the feminine form moved towards me. I attempted to move back, but my body wouldn't move. I felt like I was pinned to the floor.

All I could hear as my vision went black was the sound of Tailen's voice screaming my name.

Chapter 11

Tailen

The weight of the catwalk hitting me was something I hadn't felt in a very, very long time. The twinge of pain that came with it was nothing I couldn't manage. I pushed the metal off me with my hands, the floor clattering in the chaos of screams was barely heard. The sigils lines had been broken.

I saw a huge amount of light come in from one of the brick walls. Sal had thrown the front end of a truck through the brick wall, his attempts to enter having been foiled earlier by the spirit holding the doors closed. My attention, however, was not on him but on the spirit lifting Mikhail from the ground, his screaming hit my ears and I felt myself snap.

Tendrils of inky black shadow shot out from around my hands. I wound them about the spirit that held onto Mikhail. He was not going to kill anyone, not anymore. I had not wanted this to get messy, but this spirit had chosen its fate. A greedy horrible man in life, and a violent spirit in death. I felt the rush of the energy as I ripped the specter apart at his torso. The remnants of his form absorbing into the shadows. I rushed forward Sal's heavy steps running up behind me.

"Mikhail! Stay with me!" I shouted at him. The flesh on his shoulder burned heavily like someone had dumped liquid nitrogen on him. His body was so cold. I shook him slightly, but to no avail. He was out, but I could feel his heart still beating in his chest. He was alive.

"Get the truck, we have to get him back home." Sal took off quickly, through the hole he had made in the wall. "I've got you Mikhail, hang on."

I picked the man up over my shoulders easily. Screw the shotgun and duffle bag, I needed to get him home, and warmed up. That wound required immediate treatment. This was my fault, and I needed to fix it. I miscalculated the strength of this spirit. I regretted my own confidence, I should have been more careful. I should have used a stronger blood, a better binding sigil. I ran from the building, Sal had pulled the truck up. I put Mikhail into the bed, and climbed in after him pulling the tailgate shut, smacking the side of the bed to let him know we could go. The trees sped by as he tried to navigate the small dirt road that brought us here as quickly as he possibly could.

I could hear groans from Mikhail's lips, which was good. I laid him on his back, putting his head on my lap, hanging on to the side of the truck bed with the tendrils that extended off of my skin. I tried to keep him steady in my lap. He was still so cold, I tore the bottom half of my shirt off, and pressed it down into the wound on his shoulder, it immediately filled with blood, but at least it would staunch it for the time being. This shouldn't have happened. I should have known better. He should not have gotten hurt because I didn't take the necessary precautions. He trusted me. I failed.

Our progress through the woods was a lot quicker out than coming in, though the ride was bumpier. I was relieved as I felt the truck's tires hit the actual pavement, and Sal hit the gas. Speeding down the road, and avoiding the town center, he knew what I meant by home. My home. Mikhail's breathing was even, though it was shallow. He had endured a great amount of pain, and now I was afraid that he wouldn't warm up. We had to get him warmed before the chill got too much for his internal organs. I could see the sun getting lower in the sky as we headed towards my cabin. My mind was filled with dread.

Sal's truck skidded in front of the cabin, and he jumped out of the cab. Helping me pull Mikhail out and getting him situated over my shoulders to carry him up the stairs. Sal pushing the door open to the cabin. I walked to the bed, putting the man down on his back on the mattress as gentle as I could.

"Boil some water, we are going to need a compress for this burn, and tea if I can get him to wake up." Sal nodded and jumped into action.

"You think he's ready to see you like this, Tailen? You won't be able to camouflage that quickly." The clinking of glass told me he found the tea and poultice jars on the shelves.

"He will just have to deal with it, yeah? I have better things to worry about than him being put off by how I look."

I chose to hide myself under a masking sigil most of the time. It made my appearance easier to digest for humans. My hair was long and black, it reached well down my back. My skin was paler and more of my tattoos were visible, all sigils of different significance. On my pale skin, the black tendrils moved around, under the tattoos but on top of my skin. They were like shadows, wispy and thin unless I bound them together off of my body. My black eyes shown no reflection or shine. My teeth were sharper. I had a very small amount of control over how I physically looked, but I used the ritual to make it easier. It had limitations of course, since I broke it, I would need time before I could cast the spell again.

I started to pull off Mikhail's shirt, the fabric had been burned away. It was strange that he was still breathing so easily. Though his skin was as cold as ice, his heartbeat was strong. The wound looked horrible. I tried to keep myself on task, getting him undressed. I pulled off his boots, undid his belt, and his pager was completely fried, his handgun still freezing cold, this was not the way I wanted to see him naked. I removed his pants, tossing everything into a pile on the floor. I started covering him up with blankets, the sound of the whistling kettle meant that the poultice would be ready soon.

I layered as many blankets as I had on top of him, leaving the shoulder exposed so we could clean it and apply bandages.

"I can take care of his wound Tailen, go make the tea." Sal came to my side, stirring a thick paste in a bowl, he had tea towels tossed over his shoulder. I allowed him to start cleaning the wound, and apply the bandage to it. I was feeling a bit defeated, and Sal knew that. He was a good friend, and I'm not sure what would have happened if he wasn't there to help get us back so quickly.

I went about mixing the tea I wanted, it would hopefully stave off the cold he felt. As well as encourage his body to fight off infection. That would be the main concern while the burn healed. I set the cup next to the bed as Sal was putting the final wrap on the shoulder.

"It cleaned up okay. It will need to be watched." He looked over to me and sighed. "I'll stay with him, you go clean up. You have blood all over your shirt and I think your hair....." He shooed me off, sitting himself down on the edge of the bed, tucking the blankets in around Mikhail.

I left him to it going into my bathroom and stripping off the clothing just leaving it In a pile under the sink. I looked at my face in the mirror, I must have rubbed it because there was blood. I stepped over the rim of the high tub, and started the shower. It was cold; I didn't care. I didn't even let it warm up for a moment before fully sticking my body under it and letting it wash all the iron shavings, dirt, and blood from my tattooed skin. I sometimes thought that a good hot shower could wash away more than dirt. Not today. The thoughts of my failure stayed with me even as I wrapped my long hair into a wet bun on the top of my head.

I took my time, knowing that Mikhail would be safe with Sal for the time being. I had been right too, as I emerged in my towel, grabbing the nearest long shirt, Sal was very carefully helping the man to drink the warm tea. I slipped my shirt over my head and Sal allowed me to take his spot, retreating to the sofa. There were no words exchanged at first, his eyes were barely open. He managed to get a few out after the tea had been completely drunk.

"I'm going to need a serious explanation when I wake up." His eyes closed. I leaned forward and put my forehead to his.

"I can do that. Just sleep now." I helped him lay back onto the pillows, and made sure the blankets were pulled up tightly around him.

I joined Sal on the couch, leaning over on his shoulder.

"He's very resilient for a human. That spirit got a good hold on him." Sal spoke softly, but there was a curiosity with which he spoke.

"I'm glad for it. I couldn't bear to lose a friend before their time. I made a mistake Sal. I should have been more careful."

"You should have, but you didn't know. We both know the spirits in the town if they can even manifest, are not strong. It's over, and done." He was right, I had been reckless but all I could do now was take care of Mikhail and deal with the consequences.

"Do you want to share a pipe before you leave? I'm sure Marcella is wondering where you are." Sal shook his head, and slapped his knees as he stood up, shifting me off his shoulder as he did.

"I'm ready to go embrace my lovely fiancee, I will be fine. Besides, I have to start my new medicine tonight, and I don't know how a smoke will interact with it."

Sal gave me a hug, I buried my face in his soft stomach. It sometimes hurt to feel things this much, failure was one of the things I disliked the most. He squeezed me tightly before leaving. I saw him rummage around in Mikhail's pants. He held up the SUV keys and then tucked them into his own pocket before heading out the door.

I returned to the side of the bed, touching Mikhail's face. He was warming up. For that I was glad, he seemed to be sleeping at least mostly peacefully.

Over the night and into the morning, I kept watch over Mikhail sleeping. I changed the dressing on his burn, keeping it moist with the poultice. My mind didn't wander far from just taking care of him. I didn't want to leave his side for longer than I had to.

Sometime in the morning Sal dropped off the SUV. The key had been slid under the door. I was grateful to him for everything. To try and pull my mind away I lit up the pipe that I kept in my leather bag. Opening a window, I leaned out of it. The bowl of the white pipe glowing red, the plant in it soothing my thoughts even if it was for just a few moments.

The plant in the pipe was known as Heilige. It grew in specific conditions and I found that it was very useful to people like me. Unhumans, Supernaturals, the Unknowns, or the plethora of what regular humans called us. The plant calmed our bodies, and could be mixed into rituals, teas, and smoke. It could be distilled into oil if given enough of it. Luckily for some reason I could grow it myself. My presence around the plant was enough for it to take root, at least in a pot.

I was lost in my mind for longer than I thought, because I was startled by the sound of feet hitting the wooden floor. I spun around from the window, to see Mikhail sitting up on the edge of the bed rubbing his eyes with the palm of his hands. I dropped the pipe in an ashtray on the window sill and practically ran to him. Touching his non-burned arm.

"How long have I been out? I feel like a truck hit me." He let his hands fall away, and opened his eyes looking up at me, and pulled back, startled.

"Almost a full day…" I stepped back, looking away from him. "I'm sorry that you got injured. I underestimated how strong that spirit would have been, I should have been more careful."

"I'm still not sure what happened, shouldn't I be dead? And what happened to you." The last half pinged my emotions a little bit. I must have shown it on my face. "You look different, I'm just trying to make sure I'm not seeing things. You only had a couple tattoos before." He was trying to be kind to me even though I felt it was undeserved.

"You are resilient apparently. The spirit did manage to do some serious damage to your skin. I wouldn't look under your bandage just yet. As for me, I'm not sure what you want to hear. I've never been good at hiding myself for long." Mikhail reached out towards me with an open hand, sighing deeply. I grabbed his hand and gave into its pull to sit down by him again.

"Something told me that you were not sharing everything with me. I'm not sure if I should be angry or just irritated. This whole trip up here has thrown my world view into question, and I'm too mentally exhausted to fight it." His eyes gazed down at the floor, his fingers stayed wrapped around my hand. "I also know that this isn't quite over yet, and even though mistakes were made, and even if that spirit wasn't our killer, he certainly didn't need to be roaming around up there. If I had been a hiker that stumbled on that place...." His voice trailed off.

"It's not over, and if you want me to explain, I will. I don't like hiding behind a mask, but it's necessary most of the time. Almost all the time. It's easier for me to navigate among humans. Think of if Sheriff Southland caught wind." I heard a chuckle from him, shaking his head.

"He was right about you not being human. Though I'm not sure he's right about you being a menace." Freeing my fingers from him he pushed up to standing, I reached up to stop him from falling as his knee gave out slightly. "If you want to talk, we can do it while I take a shower. I feel like that spirit left residue on me, it's sticky feeling."

"That's the poultice we put on your burn. Best you sit down in the bath, don't want to get the dressings too wet." I stood up, tucking myself under his good arm. I helped him get into the bathroom, and he waved me off.

"I can get myself in the bathtub." I was going to protest, but I figured out what he meant pretty quickly.

I gave him space, shutting the door behind me. I decided that while I waited I would get the bed stripped down and remade. The sheets had gotten some blood on them, not to mention the dirt and iron from the foundry floor. I shoved them into a hamper, and found new ones in a basket that was under the bed. They were black, and a bit faded, but soft. Hopefully I would be able to convince him to rest more once he was clean. I checked the blankets making sure they hadn't also gotten soiled too.

I heard the bathwater start up and a loud thunk. I assumed he sat down a little hard in the tub. I checked myself before going to the bathroom. I had on my over sized shirt and underwear, which should, in my mind, be good enough to help him get a bath.

I pushed the door open to the bathroom. He had figured out the tap, and was laying back with his head against the wall, eyes closed. I could see the steam coming up from the water, it was quite hot. I sat myself down on the side of the tub.

There was a little bit of tension in the air, as the sound of the water was the only thing to be heard. So, I decided that someone had to break it.

"Where do you want me to start." I reached for the tap, turning it off as the water reached its max in the tub. Mikhail's eyes remained closed but he shifted in the water a bit, getting comfortable.

"Where are you from?" That seemed like an oddly mundane question, but I knew what he meant.

"I was pulled here from across what most refer to as the Veil. I was pulled into a place that is now called Denmark?" I could barely remember that far back in my memory. For me it was a strained part of my psyche, it was full of too much bitterness and death to really want to push myself to think about it in detail.

"You were pulled here? Unwilling participant?"

"I would say that unwillingness is an understatement. I have accepted my place here in this world. I do not wish to return to where I was before this. It is too beautiful here, there is so much color, I am fascinated by the resilience of humanity and want to be part of it." It was an untenable truth of my existence. All I wanted was to live. "But yes, I was not asked if I wanted to be ripped away from my family. From my kind."

Mikhail opened his eyes to look at me, his eyes narrowed slightly as his eyes traveled up my arm to my face, locking with the blackness of my own eyes. It made me wonder what he was thinking. I wasn't ashamed or had unfavorable self-confidence about how I looked, I always just chose to look as human as I could for the ease of others.

"Are you a demon? I don't think I have ever seen eyes like yours outside of movies." I laughed, a loud laugh. If I had kept count of the times I was asked that question, I could fill the town library's archive with scrolls.

"Some may call me that, but I can tell you that I am not. Truthfully demons and I have little in common besides some sharing my ocular affinity. I don't know if I should be offended." He made a displeased grunt, and tried to push himself up to a better sitting position. "It's not easy to explain, I am better at showing." Mikhail seemed more pleased with that. "My kind has had many names over the years. Leviathan, Old Ones, The Darkness, and I am pretty sure that one ancient text referred to one of my brethren as a large black squid." I allowed the tendrils of shadow to drift along the sides of the bathtub. Mikhail only gave them cursory glances as we continued to speak.

"I'm learning a lot more than I would have liked on this trip." He tried to reach for a wash cloth on the far edge of the tub and winced. He made a defeated face. "At least I have an explanation why you seem a lot stronger than you look, also, no offense...you are weirdly heavy."

"I forget that my body is so small sometimes. This human body just houses me. I'm quite a bit bigger than my body lets on." He was taking this all surprisingly well, though he was trapped in a bathtub currently. "Can...can I help you?"

Mikhail nodded, I helped him move forward in the bath, scooting around towards his backside. I swung my legs into the tub, my feet splashing down into the water. I steadied myself on the back edge of the tub, reaching to the small shelf over the tub for the cup I kept there. I started to carefully pour water over his hair, it was filthy and full of blood.

"What actually went wrong in there Tailen? I thought you were crushed. I saw that metal plate crush you." He leaned his head back so the water flowed off his hair and down his back. I took the shampoo and ran my now soapy hands through the longer hair on top of his head. "I assumed we were both dead."

"There isn't much that can hurt me. Least of all a heavy object or an angry spirit for that matter." I sighed deeply as I scrubbed the blood and dirt from his sandy brown and grey hair. "I underestimated the fortitude of the spirit. He held enough vengeance that he could affect the world around him. I thought he hadn't gained enough strength. I should have used a stronger spell. I was too confident. I didn't account for him being murdered, well potentially, by his workers. I have feeling that his arrogance in life is what translated to all that rage I felt from his spirit." My voice trembled slightly as I thought about what would have happened if I hadn't been as strong as I was. I felt Mikhail's hand grasp mine for a moment. Even now, he tried to comfort me.

"We are alive, for now. I'll take that. Neither of us knew what we were walking into. You are not alone, I could have spoken up. My trust in you was not unwarranted, and in the end we are here." He let me go back to washing his hair, I enjoyed the feeling of his form under my fingers. Maybe more than I deserved to at this moment.

"I do not deserve your kindness. You should have never been injured so badly. Mikhail..."

"It's not kindness. It's truth. I'm angry. Not at you. I'm angry that something got us to this point. Though, right now. I think I want to enjoy you washing my hair."

His body leaned back, his wet head landing on my stomach, looking up at me. His tired eyes, half closed, seemed at least mildly contented. I poured some water down his chest, following it along with my free hand, letting it rest there as he closed his eyes letting out a deep sigh.

I did wish he was not injured, but I would not complain about the naked man resting against me.

Chapter 12

Mikhail

My shoulder hurt, but it was an ache. Not like I would think a burn should hurt. It must be the poultice that Tailen had been dressing my wound with. When I had woken up my body felt so heavy, but after sleeping in relatively dreamless darkness for almost a full day, that was to be expected.

As I sat in the bathtub asking my questions, I could feel the distress coming off of Tailen. I was angry, but not with her. It was more of a mental pain when it came to her. Like she was hiding from me. It was a lot to process admittedly, but I dealt well with change. My life had prepared me for sudden twists and turns. I just wanted to know why. I could tell she was answering me honestly, I suppose I couldn't blame her for not wanting to announce herself to the world as a non-human, especially not in this small town. I did wonder what would have brought her here. Seems like it would be a stifling place for someone like her.

I was not lying when I said I enjoyed her fingers in my hair. It was strange that a woman with such raw strength could run her hands over me with such a delicate touch. I had to fight off the insecurity I had with the injury, and allow myself to just let her take care of me. As my head laid back on her shirted torso, she didn't even complain that I was making her clothing wet. Just continued to wash the dirt from my skin. I felt the need to ask her more questions about herself. Probe for more.

"Will you tell me more? Not now, but when we are finished, I don't mean with just the bath." I shifted forward again, rubbing my legs with my soapy hand on my good arm.

"I wouldn't have ever not answered you honestly. No one asks the questions though. I will answer whatever you want." She dumped one last cup of water over my hair. I felt her stand up in the water, stepping out of the tub. I gripped the side wall, and pushed myself to stand, her hands helping me get up without falling. I noticed she averted her eyes to the side.

"I think I can manage on my own for a few." She handed me over a towel. I wrapped it around myself to dry, watching her walk away back into the main room in her damp oversized shirt. It just occurred to me that she had her bare legs basically wrapped around me for the last half hour.

After drying myself as much as I could. I returned to the living area. Tailen was puttering around in the kitchen. I remember her feeding me some tea, and that was what I was smelling once more. I searched for my clothing, but all I found was the haphazard pile of my torn garments laying in a pile near the bed. So I sat on the edge of the bed, hips wrapped in the towel. I noticed that the afternoon sun was coming in the window, though it was beginning to darken by the minute.

"There is a storm rolling in, I can feel the static in the air." Tailen commented as she came to me holding a steaming cup. "Drink this. It will help with the healing, and staving off the cold. Though you seem to be doing that alright on your own."

"I'm not going to lie; it sounds better than coffee currently."

"A core of your personality, shattered."

"It's not a ...yeah, yeah it is." I sipped the tea she handed me. It was sweet, honey if I was picking it up correctly. It hit my throat and sent a warm feeling through my body. It was quite good even if it was bitter on the back end. I didn't dare ask what was in it. Didn't need to learn more today. Tailen walked over to a small dresser and began to rifle around. It took her a few minutes before she returned with a pair of flannel soft pants. They looked a bit small for me.

"They are Sal's but they shouldn't be too bad. He left them after hunting one time." I shrugged and stood up. I let the towel fall from my hips as I stood. Tailen looked away again, we were literally just in the bath together, yet she wouldn't look at me. Why?

I pulled on the pants; they were a bit snug in the butt. Also, really too short. I felt a little silly in them. Tailen did let out a little bit of a laugh as she turned back to me. I sat down, and the legs almost raised up to my knees.

"Let me...let me redress the wound." She was clearly stifling her laughter.

I stayed seated on the edge of the bed as she peeled off the dressing. I wondered if I should try to look at the wound, but Tailen used her finger to turn my chin back away. I had seen burns before, but it may be a bit different to see them on yourself. It stung a little as she cleaned it, and slathered on what felt like a thick paste. I assume it was the poultice. It made the sting subside, and strangely the ache was all that was left. She finally allowed me to look at it once she got the bandage tied back over it.

"You should rest Mikhail. I know you probably want to..."

"I will, I'm not feeling like going back to that motel room. To be honest, I'm not sure if I want to be alone." Well that just came out of my mouth, but she didn't say a word. She just gently pressed my good shoulder back towards the bed.

I laid back, and she covered me. I grabbed her wrist as she finished. So she followed, her shirt still damp from my hair, she laid on her side next to me. Her hand rested on top of the blankets covering my chest. I'm not sure how long it took me to fall asleep but it felt instantaneous.

It was a few hours later when I awoke to the sound of thunder crashing outside. The wood of the old cabin creaked and yawned as the wind and rain beat against the outside of the old structure. I no longer felt the weight of Tailen's hand on my chest and I searched for it. I sat up, it was feeling easier now. I scanned the room. There sitting in the window sill watching the storm was the long-haired woman for whom I searched. The lightning lit her up in silhouette, it almost gave me a flash back to the previous day of her in the factory.

I rolled myself from the bed, moving and stretching my injured shoulder. Tailen turned to look at me. Moving from the window sill she set down a pipe, the red glow was really the only light in the room. Though that was quickly remedied by her lighting a hurricane lamp sitting on top of her old television.

"I thought you would be sleeping Tailen. The storm keeping you up?" She shook her head, that long black hair looked so shiny in the lamp light. She had changed from the oversized shirt into a black thick robe that touched the floor.

"I don't find sleep easy. I was asleep for a very long time...and storms are meant to be witnessed." Her tone was low, her unplaceable accent seeming more pronounced when she spoke softly.

I moved to the sofa, pulling the legs of these silly pants up so they didn't choke my calves. Sitting down and watching the strokes of lightning cross the sky through the window. I couldn't argue with her. The majesty of nature was impressive. I could almost feel the static in the air. It seems the storm was fairly close to the cabin.

"I would say you might find something in common with a storm of such magnitude, yeah?" This seemed to give Tailen pause as she came to sit by me.

"That would be a better description than demon, yes." Her eyes seemed trained on the lamp light. When I looked at them, it was like a void, unlike most people's eyes, hers did not reflect back the flicker of the flames. I knew in the back of my head this shouldn't be something that intrigued me. It probably frightened most people. Which is why she covered herself with those brown deep walnut colored irises usually.

I reached a hand to her, letting my fingers fall into the long hair that cascaded down her shoulders and pooled near her hips. Though she pulled away.

"Just the other day, you told me to...not make it weird. Now you're pulling away from me, you won't hardly look at me. Why?" I was going to get an answer, and if needed I would pull out her promise from the bathroom.

"The other day, I didn't just almost get you killed Mikhail. I have enough control to let you rest." She turned her face towards me, seriousness in her voice.

"I never said you had to control yourself."

"I can read the room. You're injured. It's my fault. Why would you even..."

"Then actually read the room."

"I am not..."

"I'm not arguing with you about this. Be my distraction from the ache in my shoulder, and let me distract you from those thoughts in your head." I reached for her again. My fingers finding their way into her soft hair, to the back of her head pulling her towards me. Her lips curled into a small smile.

"I can do that." Her body shifted on the couch, her legs flipping over mine. Her hand going to my face, running along the scruff of my cheek. "Just don't hurt yourself."

"Oh, there is plenty I can do with just one good shoulder Tailen." I felt her breath on my face just before I pressed my lips against hers. Her body shuttered slightly under the grip of my good arm that had snaked its way behind her back. Her lips parting and letting out a moan into the kiss, my tongue pushing into her mouth. She tasted like earthy smoke and honey.

I pulled away from the kiss, panting. My hand gripped her thighs that were thrown across my lap. Her tattooed skin showed as the fabric of her robe had shifted. I had almost forgotten how heavily tattooed she was, and the shadow like tendrils that moved about on her flesh. I wanted to see more of her. I needed to see more of her. Tailen's hands gripped at my chest; I could feel her lips kissing on my neck. Her fingers finding the right places to dig into my chest. It was driving me crazy. I felt her teeth graze my good shoulder. They felt sharper than I remember from our kiss at the motel. I couldn't take it anymore.

I pushed her legs off my lap which caused her to pull away, but it was just so I could stand. These stupid fucking pants. I would deal with them, after I dealt with the robe covering Tailen. I looked down at her on the couch, her face was flushed. Her eyes half closed. I leaned using my good arm to brace against the back of the couch. Roughly kissing her, which was met with just as much force back. Her tongue forcing its way between my teeth to tangle with mine. Fuck she tasted good. I ran my hand up the flesh of her thighs, and found the tie of her robe sitting just above her hips. It didn't take any effort to tug the knot free. I greedily pushed the fabric away from her. Pressing my hand into her stomach, and then up her chest as I pulled away from her lips to take a ragged breath.

Looking down at her pale tattooed skin. In the lamp light she looked like a painting against a backdrop of black. My hand on her chest circled around her breast, thumb circling her hardening nipple. The soft moaning noise she made, went right to my groin. I had to taste her.

I fell to my knees in front of her. Quickly wrapping my good arm around her back and pulling her forward, my lips finding their way to her breast. I ran my tongue across her nipple, flicking it with the tip of my tongue, before taking it into my mouth fully and sucking on her tender sensitive flesh. I heard her cry out in pleasure, her arms now free from the arms of the robe and clutching the back of my head. These damn pants were feeling even tighter. I sucked on her nipple, my free hand finding its way up her thigh. I could feel the heat from beneath her underwear as my fingers glided along the outside of the thin fabric.

Pushing aside her panties, allowing one of my fingers to slide into her warm folds. I should have teased her, but I couldn't wait to sink myself into her. I had to know what she felt like. Tailen's back arched as she let out a deep moan. This was exhilarating. My lips left her chest, so I could look up at her face, which was oh so beautiful in the light. Her parted lips were so enticing. I slid another finger into her, pushing my thumb against her clit. The small gasp she let out told me everything I needed to know. I moved my fingers around inside her, twisting, stroking, pumping, gradually getting faster....my eyes gazing up at her face watching as her moans grew louder. Music to my ears.

Tailen let out a small whine as I pulled my fingers from her, as if I had done something wrong. I slid her fingers into my mouth, tasting the sweet tangy wetness on them. I pulled at her thighs slightly causing her to slide down on the couch. Her fingers fell from their grip on my hair.

"Hips up." Without any more instruction her butt lifted from the couch and I was able to slide her panties off her. I realized that throwing her legs over my shoulders and burying my face in between her legs was not an option she would allow me. How frustrating. I weighed my options quickly, because tasting her was my only goal. I had already had one taste and I wanted another.

I pulled Tailen as close to the edge of the couch as I could, sinking down into my knees as far as I could go. Pushing her thighs wide, I saw her fingers grip around them. I smiled, she knew what I wanted. I only wished that it was brighter in here so I could get a better view of her slit. The lightning strikes outside the window only showed me that her thighs were glistening wet. I ran my tongue from her knee all the way up to the crease of her leg, stopping short of the folds of her vagina. Letting my breath tease her, barely letting my nose touch her quivering wetness.

" Mishaaa..." her voice whined.

I gave in.

Pushing my tongue into her slit, tasting her, I moaned internally, the rush of her pulsing muscles was causing my brain to almost short circuit. I ran my tongue along her inner folds, stopping to suck on her engorged clit. Flicking my tongue a few times, but returning to the long strokes with the flat of my tongue. I noticed her getting louder as I did the full tongue strokes across her clit. Finding a rhythm in it I continued to stroke her. As I felt her hand reach back into my hair, her one leg draped over my good shoulder. I pressed on teasing and licking her, finding the sweet spot where she moaned and pushed her hips against me. I wanted to hear one of her loud gasps again badly.

I pulled my lips away from her, long enough to plunge two fingers into her pulsing wetness. I got what I wanted. That loud gasping for air moan that triggered my whole body. I fell back to her clit with my mouth. I felt her starting to tense up. I pushed my fingers into her as far as I could. It was then I could see, inky black tendrils wrapping themselves around my arm. All I could feel though was pressure. I must be doing something she likes. Her hand on my hair tightened and pulled. Then she stopped breathing for a moment. I pressed further into her with my tongue, fingers pumping rhythmically and as deep as I could into her. I heard the gasp of her release. The muscles tightening around my fingers, I could barely move them she clamped down so hard. The tendrils that had been sneaking around my arm retreated back onto her skin.

Tailen scrambled to pull me up, I obliged wholeheartedly. One knee between her legs as I roughly kissed her on her moaning lips. The wetness of her orgasm clinging onto the scruff of my face. She didn't seem to mind, as she licked my jaw, and up to my ear. I was a little out of breath as she pushed me to the side so I was sitting on the couch. Swinging her legs over my hips, I instinctively grabbed her waist as she pressed her body into mine. I could feel the dampness of her wet womanhood pressing down on my cock through these awful leg prisons.

She didn't even ask me to take them off. I just heard fabric rip as her fingers clutched the waist band. They tore away like they were made of tissue paper. My hard cock now pressed against her stomach. I felt her hand go down to grip it. She took it firmly, stroking it with her fingers. As if she was sizing it up, her body looked flushed, her lips still parted slightly panting. Her hips lifted up over my lap, her hand pressing my cock back, I could feel the wetness of her pussy coating my head. I thought she would tease me, at least a little. I was wrong. Tailen came down onto my shaft fully, hard, and fast.

I let out an audible hard moan. My fingers gipping into her thighs tightly, I buried my face into the crook of her neck, breathing heavily. Her body sliding against mine with each time she stroked me. Hips lifting and pushing back down. I once again could see out of my peripherals the tendrils of shadow pooling out from her body, bleeding onto mine. Adding a strange pressure sensation that I was not angry with. I slid one hand from her hip up her side, finding its way to her chest. Tailen's breast fit my hand easily. My thumb flicked across her nipple. Her moans filling my ears, I pulled my lips back from her neck, opening my eyes watching her body jolt with each time she came down on me. The strokes were rhythmic now, plunging as far as she could take me in. I could feel my muscles tightening, as my climax neared.

I let my hands fall back to her hips, fingers gripping hard into her flesh. My head laid back into the couch, a deep guttural moan escaping as I let loose inside of her. I felt her tighten around me. The walls of her pussy squeezing my cock, as she came too. Her loud moan of pleasure echoed off the walls of the wooden cabin.

She started to slow, and my head fell forward into the crook of her neck. Breath coming into my lungs hard and labored. Her body weight felt good against me. I wrapped my arms around her middle feeling her chest heaving against mine.

This was better than any distraction I could have ever asked for.

Chapter 13

Tailen

I laid on Mikhail's shoulder on the couch. After pulling my robe back on. My breathing and his finally had normalized, his arm around my back, thumb rubbing my arm. The tension of the day seemed to have dissipated, at least for now. I had craved the touch of another but I had underestimated how much until now. Since waking up from my long stint asleep, I hadn't had this kind of touch. The embraces of Rose and Sal were good, but it wasn't the same.

"Why did you come here Tailen?" Mikhail's voice brought me out of my thoughts.

"I needed a place to recover, where I would be left alone. This place is unique in that all of the natural mountains, the iron, the lake...it deters a lot of things. Up until Sal rolled iinto to town about six months after me, it was pretty quiet here. Then again with the murders." I felt him shift and when I looked up, he looked mildly confused.

"Sal? I assumed he was from here, and also what?"

"He came here trying to find a place like I did. Away. It took me a month to pin him down before me and Rose could give him one of these to help." I gestured to one of the sigils on the middle of my chest. "I thought you didn't want to learn anything new."

"I get the feeling that I don't really have a choice in the matter. Is Sal also like you?"

"Hardly, he's a bit more canine." I chuckled a little and settled my head back down into his shoulder. "Sal was bitten and turned into a Werewolf a few years back, from what he told me it was on purpose, but the pack he was in wasn't exactly helpful in teaching him how to control himself during the full moon. Luckily, he never hurt anyone too badly, I don't think his heart could have taken it, but sure as hell scared some tourists."

"That explains all the hair." I felt Mikhail's chest rise and fall with a deep sigh, and then a yawn.

"You should sleep, unfortunately there is still work to do."

"Will you stay with me? In the bed I mean." I couldn't say no to such an earnest request from him. Though, I found sleep to elude me most nights. I nodded. "We can talk about the tentacle things later." I couldn't help but chuckle lightly. I suppose it would be something different for him, to have them squeezing him while we were intimate.

It wasn't long before I found myself under the quilt of my bed, the man breathing heavily under my head on his chest. I wouldn't find slumber, but I didn't mind listening to his heartbeat. As well as the storm still raging outside. It was close now, and the thunder shook the cabin.

The touch of others has always been something I craved. Maybe it was just my time on this plane, or a left over from when I was so close to my brethren across the veil. Either way, I found the affection of those close to me important, and I hadn't allowed myself this sort of closeness since before my last long deep sleep.

The loud ringing of my phone as the sun poured in my windows stirred me from my thoughts, though Mikhail seemed like he didn't even hear it. I pulled myself unwillingly from under his arm to go answer it.

"Tailen." Rose's voice sounded overly annoyed. "I have this FBI agent standing in my cafe, who is beside herself. She claims she cannot get ahold of Agent Lewis and apparently one of deputies sent her over here since they know he comes here for coffee."

"He's here. His pager got fried, he's still sleeping. I'm guessing it's a woman named Charlotte?"

"That's the one, wait...he's sleeping.... I'm going to need details." Her tone was like she had never been annoyed with me. "I can give her some breakfast, just get here before she loses it. You would think these Feds would have more composure."

"I will fill you in later, Rose. I'll get him up."

As I hung up the phone, I could see him walking into the bathroom. I couldn't really make out the scarring on his leg last night, but it covered almost his entire limb. That had to have been painful. Must have been the scar from the military operation he didn't like talking about.The door shut to the room before I could get a good look at his rear.

I found the robe that had been discarded the night before. Problem was he didn't have anything to wear. I knew that Sal said he would drop off the SUV, maybe there was something he kept in his vehicle that would suffice until he got back to the motel. I busied myself making coffee, knowing that he would want some before heading out.

"Tailen, can you tell me why my shoulder is healed? Shouldn't there still be...a burn?"

I swung around as he approached. The bandage that had covered his shoulder now removed, in the place of the burn was a scar. I was confused. Even with the poultice, he shouldn't have been healed so quickly. I shook my head.

"I said you were resilient, but this is not...normal." I reached for it, running my hand over the scarred area. He looked mildly uncomfortable.

"It still aches. Are you sure it wasn't the stuff you put on it?"

"It's possible. Sal may have added something of his own to it." Something was a little strange about it, but that would have to come later. Right now, as much as I hated to say it, he needed pants. "Do you happen to have anything in your car to wear? Rose called; your partner seems to be looking for you."

"I may have some of my workout clothes in the trunk. I didn't know she would be coming so soon, or at all...but I didn't get a page."

"It's fried. The cold from the spirit fried it." I let my hand linger on his shoulder for a moment longer before heading out to the car to dig around in the trunk of the SUV.

I made sure to grab the keys from the counter where I had tossed them, and went to the car, getting into the trunk hatch. There was a small plastic crate in the back. It did in fact have a pair of sweatpants, FBI shirt, and some extra magazines for his handgun, along with some discarded paperwork. I looked out into the wooded area that surrounded the house, it seemed a bit more peaceful today for some reason. Maybe because of the weight that had been lifted since last night. Though I still felt badly about Mikhail being injured, but I would not allow it to rule my thoughts.

I tossed him the clothing once back inside the cabin, as he sipped his coffee, leaning against my counter. I found it hard to peel my eyes away from him looking so comfortable and so deliciously naked. Though, I was still confused about his rapid rate of recovery. I would have to ask Sal about the poultice he made. I heard him mutter a thanks as I went to my own dresser. I chose a pair of lighter denim cut off shorts and a cropped black shirt. It wasn't until I was getting dressed that I remembered that I had to make myself more presentable to the townsfolk.

I placed my hand over a sigil on my shoulder. Enough time had passed, and I could recast the spell. Lowering my head, I spoke softly the words to activate the incantation that would hide my tattoos, and the shadows that crawled along my skin. As I spoke the ink faded into my flesh as did the shadows leaving only a few tattoos on my shoulders and back, my hair shrank back. I opened my eyes and the blackness retreated into the center of my now walnut eyes. It was at this point I noticed Mikhail staring at me from the kitchen area.

"That was not how I expected...I don't know how I thought you did that." He finished slipping the shirt over his head, covering up his delightfully hairy torso, that let out a hungry grumble that I could hear across the room. I ran my hand through my hair, pushing the now much shorter locks back, though it flopped over to one side covering my one eye.

"You are already going to make people talk coming into town wearing sweats and boots, I don't need any more attention than I already draw." I grabbed my bag and threw it over my shoulder, making sure to pack my pipe, and the small journal that I had picked up at the factory. I would take it with me to the library. I needed to look over it. "That is if you will give me a ride into town with you."

"I'm not sure that I prefer you without all your tattoos, Tailen." Mikhail met me halfway to the door, after gathering his things from the heap I had left them on the floor. "I'm not opposed to the company, plus your bike is still at Sal's, and I really need breakfast. I have been so out of it that I haven't eaten."

I nodded in agreement. It wasn't too long before we were on the road, headed back into town. At some point I noticed that he had slipped a hand over the center console of the car and found a way onto my thigh. I found comfort in his touch. I liked the feel of his calloused fingers on the skin of my leg.

"I must say Mikhail, that you have been taking everything in stride. Just the other day you were telling me you don't believe in spirits, yet...here you are." I slid my hand over his, though my eyes stayed trained on the woods and the passing tourist signs alongside the road.

"Believe is not the correct word. I guess, I didn't want to accept the things in front of me. There are a lot of things that cannot be explained. I handle change fairly well. I won't lie to you and say It's not confusing or scary, but I have to accept it." I could hear hesitance in his voice. He was thinking of something hard again, like when he briefly spoke of the time in the military. I wouldn't push it. In time maybe he would share more.

"I've been around for a long time, Mikhail, and there are still things that I don't understand. I do know that at least I don't frighten you."

"Oh, I didn't say that. You scare the living shit out of me. So does Rose." He paused. "Don't tell her I said that. I think she would like it too much." I laughed loudly. He was right, she would like that a bit too much. He was right though; she was a terrifying woman. In the best ways. "I know it's not polite to ask, but how long have you been around?"

"Longer than some lakes, and shorter than some mountains." I chuckled. He grunted in a disapproving manner, but didn't press any further. He would get his answer at some point. I doubt he would let my non-answer slide for long.

The SUV pulled up in front of the cafe. I could see it was a little light on customers, which was probably a good thing considering. I could see the outline of a woman in a suit sitting at one of the tables. Mikhail grabbed the door before I could, and touched the small of my back as I walked in past him. It was then I heard an unfamiliar woman's voice with a light Midwestern accent.

"You look like you got hit by a truck Mikhail." The voice came from the suited woman at the table. She stood up from the breakfast at her table, straightened her jacket, and cocked her head to one side. "I was about to call for a search party, no one heard from you for a couple days."

The woman was very neat, unlike Mikhail when he was in his suit. Hers was pressed; her white shirt buttoned all the way up to her neck. Her blonde hair pinned back into a bun; hair slicked back away from her face. She had fair skin, and some freckles. A small amount of eyeliner and mascara on her blue steely eyes. She stood slightly shorter than myself and Mikhail. She looked rather annoyed and unhappy.

"My pager got fried. I didn't really have control over the last couple days. I will fill you in." He rolled his eyes and plopped down in the chair that was at her table, which she sat back down as well with a bit of a huff. "After breakfast, I'm starving, and I need more..." Before he could say coffee, the perfection that is Rose was already pouring him some, and sliding a small pitcher of cream onto the table. He gratefully took the cup in his hands.

I took my place at the counter near the table. Rose sniffed the air as she walked past me and smiled brightly. I was not completely looking forward to the discussion she was going to want me to have about my activities with Mikhail. I took my bag off and set it on the counter a cup of black coffee finding its way into my hands.

"You still should have checked in, you have an actual job to do, and usually you are all protocol this and do it right that. When I got here and you were not at the motel, or the police station...."

"Charlotte, I was working the case. It's hard to check in when the phones up here are few and far between. It's not like in the city. You know that. We made some headway..."

"We? Who is...Oh her?" I spun on the stool at the counter, to see Charlotte gesturing towards me. "Isn't this the woman who was the first person on the suspect list?"

"Miss Galloway was taken off the list the first day. I thought I added that to my notes in my first check in."

"That still doesn't explain the we." By this time one of Rose's staff had dropped off a plate with a number of savory pastries in front of Mikhail, who wasted no time digging in.

"I don't really appreciate being spoken about like I am not sitting here." I said dryly. My face held neutral as I spoke. "Agent Lewis needed assistance, since what he was dealing with was outside of his scope of expertise. I'm sure in the debrief he will explain." I sipped my coffee. Mikhail chuckled and bit into the bagel he was currently eating.

"Then I suppose I should thank you, Miss Galloway." She reached her hand across the gap from the table towards me, I reached and grasped her hand. "I'm Charlotte, I don't particularly like being called by my last name."

I felt a sting as I grabbed her hand. It was a strange feeling; I wasn't sure if I liked it. It made me uneasy. Maybe I was just feeling a pang of irritation, or jealousy. Though after all my years, it was not something I usually felt. I let her hand fall away.

"Neither do I. Mikhail said you might be joining him to finish the investigation. More hands he said." I set my coffee mug down.

"Charlotte always goes by her first name so people don't laugh at us when we introduce ourselves." Mikhail chimed in with a grin on his face. "Agents Lewis and Clark just is too much for her."

"Before we dive back into that I think he needs something better to wear than his workout gear. Where were you that you didn't have..." Charlotte seemed to ignore Mikhail's joke, getting back to the conversation at hand.

"I was out the last few days, and my normal clothing got pretty beat up. I was lucky that I had this in the car, otherwise I would be in here naked." His voice turned a little serious, and i caught a whiff of confusion in his voice. I feel as if I had missed something.

I heard Rose make a loud whistle from the register.

"Oh Agent Lewis, you shouldn't tease us girls. I would pay good money to have you sit in here in just the suit your mother gave you." Rose fanned herself and laughed that infectious laugh that caused Mikhail to blush and Charlotte to look down at her plate.

Mikhail finished up his food. I spun back to the counter to finish my coffee. Admittedly the warm cup did not do much for me beyond feel nice, and give me a sense of normalcy in such a public space. I felt Mikhail's hand touch my shoulder.

"I will check in with you later, are you going to the library? I need to get her settled in and change." I nodded and looked up to his face. He seemed a little sterner than he had on our ride over, but didn't shy away from being so close to me even with his partner standing nearby.

"That's my plan. Your partner seems nice." He chuckled and shook his head.

"She is something." His hand trailed off my shoulder as he headed towards the door. Rose shouted about him paying his tab before he left town.

The jingle of the door as they left seemed to be Rose's cue to come over and lean herself on her hands in front of me on the counter. Her bright perfect eyes just gleamed with excitement. I knew what she wanted without her even having to ask.

"Only if we go out back, I have had enough laundry aired in your cafe for the week." You would have thought I gave her a puppy for Christmas the way she squealed and happily told the waitress helping her she was taking a break. Not that she even needed to do that. Being the boss of a well-staffed diner meant she could pretty much do as she pleased. Rose just preferred to be up front and handling customers.

I grabbed my satchel and followed my friend through the kitchen, it smelled like yeast, sugar, and bacon. I sometimes thought I could just live in her café's kitchen. A burst of wind hit me as she pushed open the door to the concrete pad that extended out the back of the building. There were a couple of cars parked, probably belonging to her staff, and the metal staircase that went up to the second floor where her apartment was.

Rose sat down on the steps leading up, crossing her perfect legs and leaning back on her elbows.

"Alright Tailen, spill. I can smell that man all over you, and I saw the way he touched your arm. What did you do to that poor man?" I knew she meant it in jest, but for some reason I felt like she was asking about his injury that she couldn't even see. That bit of insecurity just sitting in the back of my head.

"We got back from the factory, he was injured, I treated his wounds, maybe helped give him a bath…" I spoke those words into the ground, as I busied my hands packing my white pipe full of the Heilige leaf.

"You may have given him a bath? From the way he looks I would guess you gave him more than a bath my friend." I lit the pipe with a match and took a long draw before handing it off to Rose.

"After he got some rest…I think he might like pussy better than your coffee Rose, the way he buried his face into me. It was like he was starving."

I'm surprised the neighboring business owners didn't come out with the howling squeal that woman let out. All the smoke in her chest poured out onto the ground around the bottom of the stairs. She always got excited about hearing others' exploits. Not that she didn't have plenty of her own.

"Tailen, I do believe he is the first I have heard of you having sex with anyone since you moved here. How long has it been? I bet you needed it." She was so wicked to me sometimes.

"Since before I slept, which started back in the late 40's." I was always fuzzy on exact dates. "I have had other things to do. Unlike you, I don't need it."

"It's not my fault that just touching arms and hugs from customers doesn't always cut it." She took another puff and handed the pipe back to me, as I leaned on the wall of the pink building. "That's a long time, Tailen. I know you were asleep, but still...almost 50 years? That's almost longer than I have been alive."

"He wasn't frightened of me either. It's not often a human isn't at least off put by the shadows." I spoke of course of the writhing shadowed tendrils that wrapped around my body when I wasn't camouflaged by the incantation tattooed on me.

"Wait, he saw you without your spell? You are very particular...you must really like Mikhail, or at least his cock." I will forever admire my perfect Barbie friend for her crass mouth when it came to sex.

"I didn't have a choice. He was going to get killed, and I felt he was owed an explanation." I leaned my head back on the wall, letting the trail of smoke find its way from my lips down my body. "I do like his company; the nice ride is just a bonus." I felt a jolt between my legs when I thought about straddling him last night.

I laughed with Rose as she basked in the delight of my so-called conquest of Agent Lewis. I'm pretty sure had I allowed her to pry deeper she would have made me give her a complete breakdown of every inch he had given me the night before.

As much as I would have loved to continue to regale her with my sex life, I needed to head to the library.

The investigation had to continue.

Chapter 14

Mikhail

I thought that Charlotte coming to aid was not going to happen, I was sure that it wouldn't have been worth the home office's time to send her. Not that I am not grateful for the extra eyes on the case, especially not after the last couple days. I had almost lost track of the time being here.

"You really should get yourself cleaned up Mikhail. You always look a bit unkempt but this is a new level." I felt like she is just trying to harass me, but it was bothersome because she had no clue what the last few days had been like for me.

"That's the plan." I responded cooly and opened the door to my SUV. "I'm guessing you plan on coming back to the motel with me? You drove up?" I slid into the seat and shut myself in without waiting for her to respond. I was annoyed. She wasn't wrong, but I didn't appreciate it being pointed out a second time.

My partner had always been the more polished looking of our duo. Though what she lacked in protocols I made up for, so one of us had to actually look the part of a standard agent. I saw her shake her head on her own annoyance and head across the street to the black sedan that I knew she brought in; the drive was too far for her proper sensibilities to want to take a bus.

The drive back to the motel was peaceful. I was left to my own thoughts of the last few days, though I didn't quite know how I felt being completely left alone with them at this point. I knew that once this was all over I would have more to deal with in my mind than I wanted. I hadn't lied when I said I deal with change well, I felt it easier to talk to Tailen than I did just rolling things around in my own head. Just thinking about the potential of going to talk to a therapist after all this gave my stomach a bit of a turn. They had been starting to require it for the agents involved in more traumatic cases.

The crunch of the tires on the gravel in front of the motel room brought me back to reality. I seemed to be doing that a lot lately when I was alone. Zoning into my own thoughts. I fumbled with the key for the room, and heard the click of Charlotte's shoes coming around the corner of the building.

"My rooms up by the office, the decor is very retro. Way too bright for my tastes." The perk of her voice was almost too much. I grumbled a little as she followed me into the room. "Aaaannd as usual your room looks like a teenager threw up his backpack in it."

"You're welcome to tidy while I clean myself up." I could hear her huff as I rifled through my duffle bag to get clean clothing. Luckily, I had packed more than one pair of pants. Which was unusual for me. Though, apparently matching socks was too much to ask for past Mikhail. I retreated to the bathroom with my pile of clothing and shut the door behind me.

I looked at my face in the mirror. I looked more awake than I had since I arrived. My scruff on my chin however was well grown out. A shave was in order and teeth brushing, Tailen had been too kind about my breath I determined. When I took my shirt off, I couldn't help but look long and hard at the scarring on my shoulder. It still felt tender to the touch, but healed. Unlike the scar on my leg; I could remember what it felt like to get this one. I had to remember not to let that happen again. The cold, though gone, made my mind shiver.

I turned my attention to getting my face clean. It felt nice to lather my face and remove the hair. Though I wondered if Tailen, like I, preferred the longer hair. The vision of her covering herself in her more 'acceptable' skin was strange to me now. Maybe because the short hair and mostly blank flesh felt like a lie to me?

It wasn't too long before I popped the door back open, buttoning my dress shirt up and leaving the top couple undone. Charlotte had indeed busied herself putting the files into piles on the table, the books Tailen had left seemed to all be stacked together.

"Well, don't you look much better."

"Thanks." I rolled my eyes and plopped myself on the end of the bed. My partner was standing in front of me, arms crossed.

"So, are you going to tell me what has gone on? Where have you been? Must be exciting if you are forgetting to check in."

"Most of that is me not wanting to step foot in the station. That Sheriff is insufferable. He grinds my gears."

"Oh, I agree. He had a lot to say about you, and your unprofessional behavior. Including you spending time with that Galloway woman."

"Don't start with that again."

"I didn't want to say anything in the restaurant, but you are not supposed to be fraternizing with suspects even if you think they are innocent."

"I don't think so. I know. She didn't kill those men; it was a spirit. We know that for sure now. What we don't know is how they got from the factory down to the crime scenes in town." I rested my elbows on my knees. Looking up at her with my brow furrowed.

"So, you are saying a spirit did all this and you have not brought in the Unknowns department? That should have been your first call." She huffed again and sat down hard in the armchair next to the bed. My eyes followed her. "You really are not acting like yourself."

"I called them, but Tailen seems like she knows more than those quacks in the basement."

"You know you are awfully defensive of that woman. What's the deal...wait..." Her eyes grew wide and her tone turned accusatory. "You are sleeping with her, aren't you?"

I stood up and paced over to the table. She wasn't incorrect, but It wasn't keeping me from doing my job. If anything, it actually helped clear my head and give my brain a break from the case.

"I'm allowed to do as I please. She's the one who got me out of the mess the other day. That spirit would have added me to the death toll without her." I ran my hand through my hair.

"Sleeping with suspects isn't part of the job Mikhail. Be-sides, I thought you were gay." Her voice was slightly raised, again with her accusatory tone. It annoyed me.

"She isn't a suspect. You have no idea what you are talking about, I will not repeat myself on that." I turned back to facing her. "Also I sleep with and date who I want. I'm

Bi-sexual. You know that. What the hell Charlotte?" This weird disrespectful comment mixed with the not telling her favorite joke about our last names at the diner, something was really off with her.

She leaned back in the chair and looked away from me.

"Fine, will you just brief me so I am up to speed, I won't bring it up again, but I'm not happy you are allowing a civilian to just dictate the case." I sighed, that would have to do. Charlotte wasn't normally like this. Maybe she was just tired from taking care of her mother over the last month. I can understand the fatigue that sort of thing can have on a person.

I spent the next while giving her the details we had: How the deaths were connected by the hiring poster, and how the demolition company had bought up some of the old mining properties, that they all were owned by the Neisbeth guy. I told her about the spirit attack. She seemed mildly unfazed by all of it. I had left out the part about Tailen not being human, and the details about the night spent with her on my lap. Though now I wished I was back there and not here.

"So, I spent a full day recovering at Tailen's from the attack, which is why I looked like I was hit by a truck, as you put it."

"Certainly isn't a cut and dry case like we thought it would be. What's the next move?"

"Tailen is going to check the archives at the library. The librarian seems to do a good job of collecting the town's history. If there were blueprints submitted to the town, they may be there, and it should give us an idea of why they were missing from the stack on the desk in Neisbeth's office. Which also means there is some sort of human element to this whole case. That spirit could not have moved the bodies. He couldn't have left the building even if he wanted to, I'm pretty sure."

"I still don't like that you are leaving things in her hands, but if you think she is trustworthy."

"I do."

"Then I don't really have a choice in the matter, do I?"

"You don't."

I was already thinking that I wanted a coffee. This talk was more stressful than it should have been. I don't remember the last time that she had been difficult to talk to. Normally she was more on board with me.

"How is your mom doing, Charlotte?" I seemed to have caught her off guard with my question, though I asked to change the subject, and I did want to know that she was doing alright with it.

"Still recovering but she wanted me to go back to work. I'm sure she will call me if she needs me again." Her answer was cut off by the phone ringing next to the bed.

Picking up the receiver, I heard the voice of one of the deputies from down at the station.

"Agent Lewis, I'm glad you are in. There has been another body found. A hiking group found it on a trail head by the lake." I pinched my forehead between my fingers.

"Are you sure it's connected to this case?"

"Yes sir. Same burns, male. The sheriff is up at the crime scene. Do you want directions?"

"Yeah, I'll be there shortly." I hung the phone up. Well shit. This wasn't good. Either the man had been dead for days, or the spirit Tailen destroyed was not the culprit. Why does it all keep getting harder? I scrawled down directions on the notepad on the nightstand. Hanging up I ripped the paper and held it out to my partner.

"Another death Mikhail?"

"Looks like it. You're driving."

As we pulled up on the scene, there were people standing behind the yellow police tape, chattering among themselves, the car parked next to the other police vehicles. I made sure I had my badge and gun situated on my belt appropriately as I exited the car. I had somewhere along the way lost my sunglasses, I wish I had them with the bright early afternoon sun shining off the nearby water.

The Sheriff was standing nearby but I let my partner go talk to him. Considering the last time we spoke it got heated, it was for the best. I approached the deputy that was standing near the body that was strewn across the dirt path.

The body of the man looked like it had been picked at by wildlife, he was like the others a bit. Looked strong and as if he worked with his hands. The telltale spirit burn was across his face. What a horrible way to go. It made my shoulder ache even more looking at him.

The deputy explained that he had been found by a hiking group made up of older men and women. They were pretty freaked out by it. One woman had said she wanted to leave if there were spirits lurking about in the woods. They had called the time of death as sometime last night, but it was hard to tell since there were clearly bite marks from scavengers on him.

I asked for a pair of gloves so I could go through the man's pockets. These ones fit better than the ones Tailen kept at her house. I pulled the wallet out of the man's pocket and handed it to the deputy, reaching over to go into his other pocket pulling out a wad of receipts and some change. I checked his jacket pockets, they like the other victims, had dirt in them, as well as his hair. He was connected, we knew that at least.

I stood up, and the deputy handed me the man's ID, he was from out of state but that wasn't uncommon for a tourist, though I didn't believe he was one. I took the wallet and handed them the wad of receipts, thumbing through the cash, the coupons, I pulled out a newish looking business card. *Old World Demolition* and the name of an apparent associate, plus the phone number we already knew. Different from our other victims, he must have been recruited for work before the others. That means...there is still work going on and it's not at the factory.

"Charlotte." I yelled over to my partner, handing the deputy back the wallet and thanking them briefly before meeting my partner halfway.

"The Sheriff can't seem to wrap his head around this one, because we know you were with Miss Galloway last night. I think he's madder that she didn't kill someone, than that a person is dead." She crossed her arms over her chest shaking her head a bit.

"I'm sure he is. The victim has a card from that demolition company I talked about. Not like the other ones, this was a business card, and he was from out of town. Not sure what that means yet." I put my hands on my hips and looked over my shoulder at the corpse being now zipped up into a body bag to be sent off the coroner's office at the hospital.

"So now you are thinking it wasn't that spirit up at the factory? So that whole endeavor up there was pointless?"

"Not pointless, but not as fruitful as we hoped." I wasn't sure why she said that with hostility in her voice.

I decided that walking the area was a good idea. Though my efforts didn't bring anything of note to my attention. Any footprints would have been obscured by the hiking group coming in that morning. There were deputies seeing if there was any trace in the area, hairs, unknown substances, clothing trace, anything that could tell us who may have dropped this man here. It was very apparent to me though, that this was a body drop. Just like the others. He had to have been killed elsewhere, but the question still remained. Why?

Charlotte followed me back towards her car. I sat back on the hood of it surveying the scene. I felt the car shift as my partner joined me looking through the notebook in her hand.

"Not much else we can do here. We should head to meet the body at the morgue."

I grunted in agreement; I couldn't help shake the feeling that something wasn't right. Hopefully Tailen would turn up something at the library. When we got to the morgue, I would have to call Marcella and relay what was going on.

We needed another break in the case. This threw a wrench I wasn't prepared for.

Chapter 15

Tailen

I left Rose with a promise to return with more details, though I would not actually be doing that. She had enough of her own exploits to enjoy. Plus, I wanted at least a little of my intimate life to be my own. At least for the time being. I wanted to enjoy the warm feelings my time spent with Mikhail for as long as I could. It had been too long. There was just something about him that sparked my interest, made me want to tease him, touch him, solve murders with him, apparently. He was a human with competency in his job, and I liked that.

The streets of the town were starting to fill back up with people again, just like they did mid-week during tourist season. It was strange that I had started to get used to it over the years. There were many points during my stay here that I spent time sitting near the lake watching people enjoying themselves on their vacations. Taking in the small things that they enjoyed like swimming with their families or fishing with their friends.

The library was quiet as ever, the sounds of footsteps and pages turning, ticking on computers, and the smell of old book pages. It was a place that I one day would miss. The old iron beams that made the frame of the building gleamed in the light streaming through the windows high on the walls.

Marcella was stationed behind her desk as usual; she was typing away at her computer, and she had a new stack of books next to her.

"Did you get a donation?" I leaned on the old desk, smiling at her. Which she knew meant I needed help.

"The school's library needed to get rid of some of their extras." Her eyes turned up to me. "Glad to see you are in one piece. Sal said you guys took a beating at that factory." Her voice felt distant.

"I'm sorry Marcella. I didn't know..."

"I know you and Sal can handle yourselves, but it's not particularly comforting having my fiancé coming home covered in dirt and telling me about a malicious spirit. He pulled a muscle throwing that truck." Shaking her head at me she stood up and reached over the desk touching my arm. "It's worry, not anger. I understand that my life got pretty complicated when I decided to say yes to marrying him."

"I appreciate that. I don't know if Mikhail would have survived without him being there to get us back." I felt her forehead touch mine and then a pinch on my cheek.

"Just no more of that please." We chuckled together and she sat back down. "Now what can I help you find, considering you haven't returned my books, I'm guessing you need something else?"

"Blueprints, mid 1960s? Do you have any old records of those down in the archives? We found some incomplete ones up at the factory office, someone clearly took some pages from the stack. I want to see what they took."

Marcella seemed lost in thought for a few moments, but her eyes lit up as if a lightbulb turned on in her mind.

"There are some boxes that were brought over when they cleaned out the offices over at the courthouse several years ago. They should still be stacked back in the corner downstairs. If not there, then up on the second floor with the microfiche machines. I had someone working on transferring them at one point but it's pretty low on the priority list." I loved it when her thick New Orleans accent had excitement twisted in it.

I waved as I headed back down to the basement. I did love it down there. It was where the smell of the old books was the heaviest. I had intended on going down there to read through the diary I had found anyway. It was quiet and cool, and the lighting though low was my preference to get stuck into pages of a book.

I found my way through the shelves, letting my fingers on occasion trail across the books and files as I made my way to the farthest end of the basement, far from the stairwell. I turned on a lamp on the line table that was against the back wall. The lightbulb flickered as it had been a while since it had been turned on. I easily found the stack of boxes; they were at least labeled. I took off my bag, and set it on the table and began my work. There was something comforting about digging into the history of a place, even if it meant going through dusty old boxes.

The boxes were unkempt, but easily gone through. It was more than I had hoped, and I increasingly understood why it was low on the list for archival. I spent time to at least open each box even if the label on the front wasn't related to what I was looking for. The cardboard squeaking as I removed the lids from the boxes was starting to get grating to my ears as I progressed through them. I almost didn't want to open the last of them, but I held a little hope that maybe I would get lucky and not find another one full of tax forms or old receipts.

That hope was dashed, as even the last box was just mostly blank old permit forms, and some magazines. I didn't like that progress had been a bit stunted, but at least I could take a moment to read through the diary.

The small book felt old; the pages were slightly brittle from being hidden away in the bottom of that drawer. The handwriting was small and clear, and the pages labeled with the dates. The man had laid out the days, in mostly formal wording, every once in a while, he would share feelings on a particular deal or his irritation with a manager.

I didn't read every page, flipping through picking out key words. There was a change in the hand writing following events that seemed to infuriate him. He had been an angry man, at least when it came to his business. The biggest change was after the mine collapse. His handwriting was messier, erratic, and filled with more profanity. He spoke of how ungrateful his workers were to even still have jobs after the mines had been shut. How the government was sticking their noses where they didn't belong. How it wasn't his fault that people didn't know how to do their jobs. Typical of a person in over their head.

Then, the last few entries. He had finally admitted to himself that it probably had been his fault. He had paid off engineers to be able to dig into unstable ground, and continue to detonate explosives, to continue the shaft that had caused the collapse. Now, his daughter who had taken an interest in learning the business was among those that had been trapped underneath the crumbling earth. Though his words didn't seem remorseful.

The very last page mentioned hiring a team to dig a new shaft. So, he could try and retrieve her body. Seemingly at the behest of his grief filled wife. I could imagine it wasn't long after he met his end, and the speculation that it was his workers, was seeming the most plausible.

As I closed the book, I stretched my arms over my head. The diary had been enlightening to say the least. It made me wonder more about those blueprints now. I couldn't quite remember, but if the dates on those plans matched with the last entries, that might be what whoever took them was after. A way to get back down into the mines. For what purpose though. Just to collect his daughter's body?

I was not looking forward to the prospect of having to go out to the mountains on the far side of the lake. That area still unsettled me.

I felt like I had been down in the basement for quite a long time. I pushed the book back into my bag. Though tedious to some, I did enjoy reading through history, even the smallest snippets of a man's life were of some interest. As I stood and threw my bag over my shoulder one of the boxes that I had opened was struck and tumbled over onto the floor.

"Shit." I bent down to start picking up the box of ledgers scattered on the floor. Though it didn't take me too long to realize something. I had never knocked anything over in this basement without the chill of Mrs. Bea's spirit coming very shortly after.

I stopped putting the box back together and looked around the room. No lights flickered, no air moved, no cold crept in. My chest felt tight. I didn't like this. I quickly ran across the basement, my feet hitting the floor heavily making more noise than I really wanted as I flew across the basement in a mild panic. I found the plaque on the wall that notated the resting place of the former head of the library. Resting my hands on it. Nothing looked disturbed.

Stepping back, I looked down at the floor, there was an outline where the floor had been replaced after the woman had been interred. I knelt down and ran my hand along the stone in the floor that covered her casket. My fingers caught something scratched on the surface of the stone. That hadn't been there before.

My mind went back to the conversation with Mikhail when he confronted me here. The spirit I had sent him to see at the cemetery he claimed had not been there. Now Mrs. Bea wasn't here.

I quickly grabbed my own notebook from my bag, the one I had scrawled rituals into. I tore the last page of the book out and laid it on the spot where I felt the grooves. Using a pencil retrieved from my bag I rubbed the graphite over the page. It revealed a sigil. One that I wasn't wholly familiar with, though it seemed to ping something in the back of my mind. I held it up so I could see it better in the dim sepia toned lighting of the basement. One thing was for sure, this had something to do with Mrs. Bea not being here.

Not knowing what actually happened infuriated me. I growled as I headed back up the stairs, I knew I was being loud. I didn't care. My mind was full of anger, and mild panic. I could see Marcella getting ready to shush the person making the noise, but her eyes widened as she realized it was me.

"What's wrong, are you okay?" She shared a bit of the panic I had in her own voice. I walked past the desk motioning for her to follow me into the hallway that led to what used to be the clergy offices.

Leaning on the wall in the hallway, I took a few deep breaths as my friend joined me, her hands gripping my shoulders.

"Bea isn't in the basement. I knocked over one of the boxes, and she didn't come to clean it up." Her fingers squeezed my shoulders and she nodded.

"I noticed she wasn't down there the other day; I thought it was just me. She hasn't always come out when I'm around. I liked to think it was her trusting me to do my job."

"I have never not seen her when I knock books over. Then I found this scratched into the stone over her casket." I held up the page, Marcella took it in her hands and leaned against the opposite wall from me.

"What is it?"

"I'm not too sure, but it's new. I have never noticed it before, and I have spent a lot of time down there, with her."

"You think this sigil has something to do with her not..." her voice trailed off.

"I don't know. I don't like not knowing. I can find out though, but I need to go to the cemetery. Mikhail had said Harold wasn't there last week when I sent him there. I didn't think too much of it, but two spirits strong enough to manifest disappearing with this case going on...something, something isn't right."

She nodded in agreement and handed me back my page.

"What can I do?" She straightened herself up, a serious look coming across her face.

"I didn't find those blueprints; do you think you can send one of your staff to check through the microfiche of the documents that have been archived? The blueprints would have been from the late 1960's possibly for a new mine shaft. Post the mine collapse, should have Neisbeths name attached to them." I didn't want to ask for her help, but I didn't have a choice in the matter, I needed it.

"You go, I will see what I can do. I'll find you when I have something. Just stay in town, okay? I'm not running through the woods looking for you." Marcellas arms went around me, embracing me. I held her back, her hair smelled like shea butter and coconut, which at least for a brief moment I found comforting. Like Sal she gave very hard hugs.

I left the library. Trying to put my thoughts in order. I didn't have my bike. The cemetery wasn't far, though the walk was something I wasn't looking forward to. Which was a strange feeling to me. I usually relish my walks and trike rides. I was nervous about what I would find at the graveyard, or what I wouldn't. I kept my pace quick, though I wanted to run, I would draw undue attention.

The cemetery was always a quiet place. It was well kept by the town, as it held some rather nice monuments and like the town center, very large old trees that provided the landscape shade. The peaceful nature was lost on me today, as my goal was to visit Harold whom I didn't expect to be there.

Usually, he was found around one of the mausoleums complaining. Though you couldn't hear him. It was like he was on a bit of a loop. If you addressed him, it would make him pause, but ultimately, he would go back into his loop of chattering about who knows what.

However, he wasn't there. I ran my hand along the top of his simple headstone. The old stone pitted from wear of the elements. I squatted down, and pushed my hair back from my face, looking at the stone's face. I sighed a bit and rested my head on the sun warmed slab. I wanted to tell the poor man I was sorry, for some reason. It was when I stood up, the sight of the mausoleum in my peripheral vision caught my eye.

On the long side of the iron and stone building was scratched in a symbol about the size of my hand. My eyes grew wide as I pulled out the sheet of paper that I had stuffed down into my bag. Turning the rubbing upright I compared. It matched one of the sigils component symbols.

I turned quickly and my eyes darted around the cemetery. My feet quickly took me across the grass and past the numerous headstones.

"No, please no." I stopped short of one of the large trees walking around it, I found another symbol scratched into the bark of the tree. It had dried sap that had oozed out caked over the spot where bark had been stripped away to make room. If this was here...then...my pace quickened as I ran towards where the next one should be. A monument of an angel, the symbol scratched into the base.

I didn't need to look further. I knew what happened here. The ritual had been extended to cover the entirety of the cemetery. Every stone, monument, and unmarked grave within the borders of a sigil that undoubtedly had already been used. A pang of panic hit my chest.

I needed to get home.

Get to my books.

I had to make a detour to Sal's garage. He had left for the day, but it was easy enough to retrieve my trike from inside the shop. I just made sure to lock everything back the way I found it. I wondered what was going on with Mikhail and his partner as I rode back towards my home. My mind had been torn from the task I had set out to do. I had forgotten to find him and check in. I didn't even check in with Rose as I rode by the front of the cafe. Too lost in my own thoughts and worry.

The warm wind of summer didn't bring me the comfort it usually did. I felt my feet dragging as I walked the stairs up into my home. The usual dimness of the room gave me little comfort. I went immediately to my bookshelves, pulling off a few old volumes of leather-bound books. I didn't want to turn on any lights, so I opted to light my lamp and I sat on the couch.

I could just faintly smell the scent of Mikhail's sweat lingering from the cushions. Though I felt no pleasure in the memory at the moment. Pulling my feet up under myself I opened one of the books, flipping through the pages, past symbols and full pages of text written in German. This book spoke mostly about rituals for protection, but I was interested mostly in the part I had turned to about protecting one from spirits. Though the sigil drawings on the page were not what I was looking for, they bore enough resemblance that I knew what book I needed to look in next.

Putting the book aside I grabbed another from my small stack, this one was older. The cover I had repaired at one time, with new leather, and stitching it to the old. I thumbed through the pages, the language was a scrawling arabic handwriting that wasn't widely used anymore, it contained theory for using spirits as energy for rituals.

I found what I was seeking. The ritual was just theory, well actually it wasn't just theory, but the book counted it as such. It described a sigil that could be used to collect and capture spirits. To use it at the scale I saw in the cemetery, was not something the writer of this particular book even mentioned.

Normally working at that scale wouldn't be very effective. Spirits normally didn't stick around their bodies for long after the body died. Here though, in this place, with spirits trapped by the soil itself, it would be astonishing the number of spirits that could possibly be drawn in and ensnared.

Someone was collecting spirits. A lot of them. I hadn't seen someone want to use that kind of power in a long time. Not since before I slept.

I shook my head to try and clear it as I snapped the book shut. Why would they want so many? I thought the days of humans trying to rip open holes in the Veil was long over.

That was the only reason I could think to need that much energy all together.

Last time that happened, I was there. I put a stop to it. Was I going to have to relive that again? Here?

I had to tell Mikhail, because if the cemetery had hundreds of souls that had already been collected there were even more under the earth of the mountain. That amount of power if used here could level this town, if not the region.

But who would want to do that? Was this even connected to the murders? It didn't matter. I couldn't sit by and watch it happen.

Even if I was wrong.

I hope I am.

Chapter 16

Mikahil

The car ride to the morgue was quiet. Charlotte didn't offer up any thoughts on the case, and seemed to be mulling things over on her own. A new body, but it didn't provide much more information than we already had. Just another pointless death. They had all been pointless.

The hospital was small, and like most of the other buildings in town, the facade looked as if it had been decades since the last update. Though, like most of the landscaping in town, it had well maintained gardens and a lawn in the front. We pulled up to the side of the building in my direction; since we would be going to the basement we didn't need to enter through the front doors.

Heading towards the back of the building, we descended the ramp that led into the basement hallway. The large metal double doors groaned and popped as I swung one of them open. A rush of cool air hit me and my partner as we entered. The hallway was long, and fairly dim. Not the comforting warm dim like Tailen's cabin that I had left earlier this morning. The morgue was about halfway down, labeled with a sign above the door which was standing ajar currently. I could hear the sound of a radio playing low talk radio as we entered. The room was colder than I had remembered from last week, but then again, it was so horribly hot out, that I didn't mind.

The coroner, a taller skinny white-haired man dressed in an open white lab coat, sat at a desk in the corner, his hand writing slowly by the light of a desk lamp. He must have heard the click of Charlotte's shoes, because he looked up as we entered the room. He spun around in his chair pushing his pen back behind his ear.

"Ah, Agent Lewis, and Agent??"

"Charlotte. I don't like using my last name please."

"Charlotte then. I got the call about the victim. They shouldn't be too far behind you. How did he look at the scene?" He leaned back in the chair, causing grating creak that hurt my ears. This was the second time she had passed up making the joke about our last names. She loved that joke.

"He looked much like the other victims." I found a place to lean on the wall. I had learned previously that he would get fussy if I leaned on his clean autopsy table. "The victim had the same burn marks as the previous, and animals got to him before he was found. Not sure how long he has been dead, but not more than a day or two." Charlotte has taken to pacing around the room, looking at the names on the body coolers.

"Animal activity say? Interesting. None of the others have had that if I remember correctly. They were found relatively quickly though." The man stroked his chin a bit before he stood up and went to busying himself getting out tools from the nearby cabinet to start setting up his trays.

I glanced over at my partner. She had finished her pacing and was now intently watching the coroner ready his tools. She hadn't seen many autopsies before, from my recollection, having only been out in the field for a couple years. I could hear the creak of the door out in the hallway and the chatter of voices coming closer. I stepped further away from the door as two hospital staff wheeled in the gurney.

With the instruction of the coroner, the men lifted and transferred the body bag onto the clean work surface. I heard the snap of latex gloves as the man prepared himself to start.

"Charlotte, are you able to assist the doctor? I need to make a call." She nodded, but looked at the man before confirming.

"She can assist. Go wash up and get some gloves on. You may want to take off your suit jacket. Grab some of the plastic aprons from the cabinet while you do." The man took no time giving her orders.

I left the room and went back to the hallway, having noticed a wall phone at the far end of the hall near the stairs going up into the main hospital wings. I could hear the sounds upstairs being so close to the stairs: beeping and the plodding of shoes on the linoleum floors.

Why was the coiled cord of this phone so long? It almost touched the floor. Seemed like a hazard to me. What did I know? I pressed zero to be directed to the operator, who connected me to the library. The phone rang quite a few times before I heard the New Orleans tone of Marcella's voice.

"Library Central Desk, how may I help you?"

"It's Agent Lewis. I'm looking for Tailen. She said she was going to be looking in the archives today." I idly twirled the cord around my finger.

"You literally just missed her, Agent Lewis. She left in quite a hurry."

"I figured she would still be stuck in the books, what did she take off for?"

"Honestly, I think she would be better to ask." She paused for longer than I liked, something felt off. "She asked me to have someone continue looking for some blueprints, but she left to go check something at the cemetery. Mrs. Bea isn't here anymore, and she is really spooked about it."

"What do you mean she isn't there anymore?"

"She found a sigil on the stone Mrs. Bea is buried under, and said she was going to check the cemetery. Like I said she would be a better one to ask. I did tell her not to leave the town though; I have to be able to find her for those blueprints."

"More complications." I sighed deeply into the receiver. "Thank you, Marcella. Can you tell her if you see her, we are at the morgue we found another body."

"Another...Yeah, I can do that. I'm sorry Agent Lewis."

With goodbyes exchanged I hung up. The click of wall phones was always satisfying. What in the world did she find now? I felt like I was behind. I was not enjoying being left in the dark. I had to remind myself that it wasn't anyone's fault that communication in the small town was slow. I really needed coffee again.

My mind went back to those first few days. I remembered her being confused when I told her about that spirit, she sent me to see at the cemetery not being there. What was his name again? Harry? Herman? Harold. That was it. Now Mrs. Bea was missing. All these names, it was almost too much to keep up with.

Entering the cold morgue again, the two of them had made quick work of opening the victim up on the table. Charlotte was placing the man's heart on a tray as I entered. I always hated watching this part. Another human be dissected on a cold table with calculated procedure. I knew its purpose and that it was necessary but it always seemed too much, especially since we knew what the man was going to say.

"Like the others, I'm confident the cause of death is from heart failure. However, the time of death. I will need a bit more time. Do you plan on waiting?" He looked at me over the magnifying lens he wore over the top half of his face.

"I would like to know as much as possible. Even if the paperwork isn't done until morning."

"Waiting it is."

The two of them went back to working on the body. I decided to post up on the wall just observing. I wondered what Tailen was on to. I would rather be out in the heat than watching an autopsy.

Time seemed to drag on, and by the time the body was being put into the cooler, I was already starting to feel the pang of hunger from not eating lunch. It wasn't unusual for me to skip meals when on a case out of the city, but for some reason it hit harder here. I'm going to blame Rose and her pastries.

"Well Agent Lewis, I will have to put time to death as Monday night. You were pretty close. Only other thing of note is that he had some pretty large chunks of iron in his chest, the teeth marks from the animals obscured an open wound. I'll make sure to add it all to the report, and keep the chunks in case they are needed. Tomorrow morning I should have it all wrapped up."

"I told him, that time is of the essence." Charlotte spoke up, snapping off her gloves and her blood drenched apron and disposing of them.

I wrapped things up with the coroner, and myself and Charlotte were on our way back into the main drag of town. I was not taking no for an answer to going to get coffee and sandwiches. Although, she didn't seem too happy with having to go back to the cafe.

She pulled the car into a space in front of the shop, and leaned on the car hood, which meant I was alone to retrieve us something for dinner. It was amazing that I could still have an appetite after watching a man getting cut apart not an hour ago. Something that came with the job I suppose. I have seen a lot worse than an autopsy before breakfast.

I was beginning to enjoy the jingle of the bell on the door of the cafe and the bright smile of the woman behind the counter.

"Well hello sugar! Taking it to go?" Her eyes looked past me out the window landing on my partner.

"Unfortunately for you, yes. Can I get a couple of those sandwiches you sent to me the other night?" She huffed a little bit in a teasing manner.

"Fine, but I expect you to come back without the wet rag so I can tease you. Tailen told me all about her nice ride." I could feel my face turning beet red. She had done her job for the day. She bounced away from me. Somehow, I feel like Rose drug whatever Tailen told her out of her, instead of the information being volunteered.

I slid my credit card across the counter to the staff member who Rose had tasked with checking me out. I made sure they added on what I owed them. Though, I'm pretty sure Rose would have let me eat for free if I let her. It wasn't long before I was presented with three coffees, a bag full of sandwiches, and from the sugary smell, donuts.

Rose leaned over the counter on her hands. Her breast always looked as if they were going to just fall out of her dress when she did that, and I swear she did it just to torment me.

"You enjoy that, sugar. Looks like I was right about needing that third coffee." She tilted her head up in a gesture towards the window. I turned to see Tailen talking with my partner. Well, I guess I wasn't going to have to wait to talk to her.

"A pleasure as always, Rose." I heard her giggle as I went back out into the street, juggling the bag and coffee in my hands.

Charlotte pulled her attention away from Tailen and grabbed for one of the coffees and the bag. The air seemed a bit tense.

"I was just filling Miss Galloway in on what happened this afternoon with finding the body out by the trail. Thought I would get a jump on it." She sipped her coffee and set the bag down on the hood of the car to grasp it with both hands, but kind of wrinkled her nose up after the first sip. "I think I got yours, it is way too sweet."

I handed one to Tailen, and traded Charlotte. She was right, it was mine. I could tell by Tailen's expression that she was not happy about something.

"I'm sorry that I didn't tell you sooner, I called Marcella but you had just left. She said you were going to the cemetery?"

"I did. I'm still trying to piece together if the sigils I found at the library and cemetery are connected to the case at all." Her explanation was short, and tone curt. She seemed almost as put off as she did the other night when she thought I might be mad at her.

"What would it have to do with the case?

"I'm not entirely sure. I really want those blueprints. Marcella said she would have Sal drive her by here to give them to me before she headed home." Again, she wasn't explaining. Maybe it was just me, but I was annoyed with the answers she was giving.

"I see. I guess we are yet again, at a standstill with the case. The only lead we got from the body was two large chunks of iron stuck in the man's chest, and the card from the demolition company in his wallet." Tailen nodded to me. Her eyes glanced over at my partner every once in a while.

"It would seem so." Why had her demeanor changed so much? Just hours ago, she was flirty and warm. Currently, cold as ice.

Charlotte pushed off the hood and grabbed the food bag, heading to the driver's side of the car.

"If there isn't anything else to discuss, I say we head back to look at those files again and get some rest, Mikhail." I nodded, and looked back to Tailen. I reached for her, laying my hand on her upper arm and leaning closer to her. Keeping my volume hushed.

"Are you alright? What's going on?"

"Something is off with her...I don't feel comfortable Mikhail."

"Are you...are you jealous?" Tailen pulled her arm away from my hand, shaking her head.

"No. I have no reason to be. I just don't trust her. How well do you know your partner?"

I was offended. I am sure it was apparent on my face as well. I had worked with Charlotte for two years now, and not once had I questioned trusting her. She did her job, solved cases, supported me and other agents. She was a model of what we should be. I was chalking up her attitude to having been with her mother for the last month taking care of her.

"I told her to give you a break, and now it's your turn. She has had a rough couple months with her mother being sick. Maybe we all just need to get some rest."

"I will come get you tomorrow when I find out what's on those blueprints."

I let my eyes linger on hers for a few moments, I found it hard even in my irritation with her to not want to kiss her. There was pain in her eyes as I broke away and went to join my partner in the car. Tailen leaned on the pink wall of the cafe, and I watched the paper coffee cup slip from her fingers and fall to the ground, spilling out onto the concrete sidewalk.

"That seemed intense." Charlotte commented as we headed back towards the motel. Holding the wheel of the car in one hand, her coffee in the other.

"Did you say something to her?" I kept my eyes trained out the window.

"I told her exactly what I said. There was a new victim, we went to the scene, went to the morgue. That's it. She is the one who seemed mad that we didn't call her sooner."

"Uh huh, she's been actively avoiding the crime scenes and the morgue. So, what did you say?"

"I may have mentioned that it was fine that she wasn't there because a civilian shouldn't be present during an investigation like that and she should be grateful that she didn't have to see the victim's maimed body."

I was not enjoying the tone of this conversation. I didn't like either of the conversations I have had in the last five minutes.

"I thought I made it clear she was helping. I don't know if you are just tired, or you are really being that big of a stickler for normal protocol, but we need her."

"You mean you need her. Not we."

I snarled under my breath a bit; the last few minutes of the ride were not my favorite. Charlotte pulled in front of the motel. The lights on the sign making the neon buzzing sound, seemed louder tonight than usual.

As I went to get out of the car I was handed the whole bag from Roses. She also leaned back to the backseat of the car, grabbing a large manila envelope, one with the string at the top that wound around to keep it closed, and handed that to me as well.

"You keep the sandwiches; I have something in my mini fridge."

"What's this?" I turned the envelope over, it wasn't labeled.

"The Unknowns Department sent it along with me to give to you. Thought you may find it interesting."

I managed to tuck it under my arm so I could handle the bag and my coffee. I wasn't sure what she would have from them, and why wouldn't they just have faxed something important. It didn't matter.

I watched briefly as Charlotte went into her own room, and I headed around the building to mine. A cooling breeze swept past; it felt good in the warm evening air. I contemplated just sitting in the grass to eat my dinner, but decided against it when I felt a fly land on my arm.

I tossed the bag of food and the new envelope onto the table. I would get to that later. Right now, all I wanted was to dig into the sandwiches and donuts. Though, after being in the morgue all day a shower sounded good before I did that.

I decided that hot water to wash away the feeling of the autopsy room was first on the list.

Too bad I didn't have someone to wash my hair for me. I couldn't help but wonder what had gotten under Tailen's skin. It worried me that she was not acting like herself. Granted, neither was Charlotte. I wonder what was really exchanged between them. They were both acting strange.

I turned the shower on to let it get hot while I stripped down. Getting under the steaming water felt good on my muscles.

Hopefully it would clear my head too.

Chapter 17

Tailen

I came back into town because of the call I got from Marcella. One of her staff had found what I was looking for already archived on the microfiche. She had them print out the pages so she could get them to me. We agreed to meet in front of the cafe. There was a weight lifted from my shoulders knowing that the plans had been found.

When I arrived at the cafe front, Charlotte was leaning on her car. I didn't think much of it at first. However, something she said didn't sit right with me. I tried to put it out of my mind, but it scratched at my memories in an unpleasant way.

After telling me briefly there had been another murder, she asked to see the scar on my side as it was partially exposed from the cropped shirt covering my chest. I had lifted it to show her the rest. I was about to tell her a white lie about it, when she spoke before I could.

"That must have been painful getting that. It always hurts worse when it's family right?"

Those words hit me in the chest as she spoke them. The unease I already felt with her grew. The clawing sensation in the back of my head started, and I was having trouble shaking it off.

I hadn't told anyone since I woke from my long sleep, who gave me this scar, or how I got it. Whoever this woman was, she was not to be trusted. It was too public of an area for me to have questioned her, or what I should have done. Which was to throw her against a wall and demand she tell me who she is. The only reason I let Mikhail leave with her, is that it would take a lot of stupidity to kill a Federal Agent. Mikhail was a capable man from what I have seen. It felt worse than I hoped watching them drive away.

I bent down to grab the dropped paper cup with its pink sleeve. I felt bad wasting it. My mind wasn't in a good place. Too much to think about. The spirits being collected, the murders, Mikhail, now a fallen coffee. I had to refocus. I had little choice in the matter. Lucky for me, the universe threw me that distraction. The horn of Sal's truck startled me.

"You okay Tailen?" I heard Marcella call out as she slid out of the truck, parked in the middle of the street. Sal's turning on his hazards. She approached me with a small stack of papers rolled up in her hand.

"Fine, I just dropped my coffee. I wasn't paying attention." I tried to put on a neutral face, though I could see concern in her eyes. Lying was never my strong suit.

"You sure?"

"I'm alright. I just need to get some more rest, I guess. All this running around the last few days has got me a bit out of sorts." I looked down to the papers in her hand, which had fallen down by her side. "Those the blueprints?"

"Yeah, you know you could come look at them at our house. I'm sure Sal might be able to help you decipher them?" I took them from her hand and shook my head. Troubling them further was out of the question.

"That's alright. You both have done enough to help. Go. Get some rest. I may need a getaway driver again." I let out a half-hearted chuckle and Marcella sighed.

"Then I'm sure Rose wouldn't mind the company." I saw her look towards the window where Rose had seemingly appeared, waving at her and Sal. I watched for a few moments as they drove away, heading towards their home.

I didn't really want to be alone, so I nodded. With a quick peck on my cheek, she jogged back to the waiting truck, yelling to call if I needed her as Sal drove down the street.

What I did to deserve friends like them since I awoke from my long slumber? I was determined to not take advantage of their kindness. I clutched the blueprints in my hand, tossing the crumpled paper cup into the trash can near the street.

I took in a deep breath before heading into the cafe. Rose greeting me at the door.

"How about you head on upstairs, and I'll be up there in a little bit. We just have to get things closed up. You know where everything is." She gave me a gentle pat on my head before puttering off to finish up serving the last of the customers sitting sparsely in the restaurant.

The apartment above the cafe, was in very stark contrast to my own living space. Though it was just as warm and cozy to me. It was very open in the main living space, mostly because it lacked a kitchen. She had opted to remove all of that at some point so she could decorate with large comfortable furniture. I flicked the lights on, which lit up several mismatched antique lamps around the space. Giving life to the color scheme of the room. It was all red, pinks, and white. The stark white walls adorned with all manner of paintings that she had collected over the years. Mostly of people in all manner of undress. Though the center piece above the large red leather plush couch was a painting of the woman herself laid naked across said couch.

The French doors that lead to her bedroom were currently shut, and the windows in the doors were darkened with a tinted film. The other two couches in the room matched the red one though were pink, and it was all arranged around a central large white coffee table, that was decorated with books and currently unlit candles. There were also floor sitting cushions tucked up underneath it. She had a couple of bookshelves filled with books and trinkets, though even those looked fairly curated and I had never actually gone through them as she always said they were just for looks. Even though it was neat and tidy like it was a magazine, I still found comfort in it. It suited her perfection.

I dropped my bag on the table and fell easily onto the red couch, letting my body sink into the squishy cushions that felt like I was being swallowed. I almost didn't want to unfurl the roll of papers in my hand to start reading them. I needed to though. I grabbed one of the matching pillows and pulled it over my lap. Setting the papers on top of it so I could read them.

They were copies printed from the microfiche machines, but the staff member who had compiled them had done a good job of making sure that they were zoomed in and clear enough to read. I was thankful for that. As I flipped through the pages, they were indeed the same as the ones I remember from the office of the factory, with some pages added. Including the top page, that had a large "rejected" stamped across the top of it. So, the inspector for the towns at the time had not approved them. Though, I am guessing that didn't actually stop Neisbeth from moving forward. From his diary, he didn't seem like a man who took "no" for an answer easily. He used to throw money at problems instead of actually doing as he was supposed to.

The front page was mostly smaller diagrams of what was later in the plans, but also had written on it coordinates to the area that was being proposed for the new shaft that it outlined. The engineer that had been contracted to outline the plans had notes on here as well. They didn't give much detail, but it did shed light on the fact that the shaft would need more reinforcement to combat the unstable land that they would be digging into. I was pulled from the documents by the sound of the door closing.

"Are you comfortable love?" Rose's voice was calmer and quieter than how she spoke during the day in the cafe. I pulled my eyes from the paperwork and smoothed them down onto the pillow.

"As much as I can be." Shifting to sit a bit higher on the couch, I slid the papers and the pillow off my lap.

"You are entirely too dressed for being in my home. I demand more comfort. Come on then." She walked over to me, reaching her hand down so I would grab it. There was little use in protesting, I would get back to my reading once she was satisfied. I took her hand and followed her to her bedroom.

Rose opened the doors to her bedroom and flicked the lights on. The room was also lit by nothing but lamps. The walls were painted a deep crimson red. In the center of the room was an overly large round bed that had entirely too many pillows in every color one could imagine, and the sheets were a silky black fabric. There were a couple of low arm chairs in the room, both facing the bed, also black, there was also a bench at the foot of it. Where she motioned for me to sit. Going to her dresser that was situated next to the door to the bathroom, she rifled around in the drawer for a moment and threw an oversized black shirt at me.

She busied herself getting undressed at her closet. On either side of that were closed up thin cabinets whose contents were not for the faint of heart. Though I was privy to that side of Rose's life, I wasn't going to go rifling through things that were not mine. As Rose shed the perfectly fitted uniform, she kicked off her shoes and placed them into their place in the closet. The uniform itself going into a basket at the bottom. Rose was such a beautiful woman to look at, even I couldn't keep myself from watching her. It wasn't lost on me why her cafe and her love life were always so full.

"Now, should I wear the black or the white...." She turned back to me, now stark naked. Though not only had she shed her clothing, she had shed her normal human colored skin. She held up two short robes in her hands.

"I will literally always say black Rose. It looks nicer against your skin." Which it did; granted she could wear a burlap sack and be beautiful.

Rose's natural skin color was like her namesake. It was a blushing pink color that was mottled with darker magenta freckles that pooled heavier around her joints, breasts, and down the middle of her stomach leading down between her thighs. From her blonde hair curled a set of rather impressive silvery horns that curled around her now pointed ears. Her eyes were a bright bold red, and flecked with black. To a human she would look rather otherworldly, as she was, but to me, she looked like my closest friend. One of the few people I could shed my own mask around.

"You are not wrong, and then we match. It's very important." She pulled the black robe around her shoulders, and loosely tied it around her middle. Placing a hand on her hip she cocked to one side. "Come on. Your turn."

I simply did as she asked, removing my clothing and replacing them with the soft t-shirt she had given me. I swear she only kept these around for me. I could feel the earnestness of her attempts to bring me back to a place where my mind was not so rattled.

We retired back to the living area, and she sat next to me on the red couch, her legs pulled up, holding a pillow in her arms. I did decline letting my hair down, as she put it, because if I needed to leave, I didn't want to do so without my sigil to camouflage myself active. Unlike her, my ability was not innate to my being. It was one of the perks of being a succubus, being able to change her appearance as wanted.

"Today has not been a good day for you. You seem rattled. I don't think I have seen you quite like this since you have arrived. Not even when we were dealing with Sal running around like a naked mad man at night."

"There have been...some developments."

I detailed my time at the library, going out to the cemetery, and what I found there. My theory on how I think someone is collecting the spirits, and my fear that something bad is going to happen. Something we won't be able to stop. How I hoped following any lead that these damn papers could give me would resolve not only the murders, but also stop the person who was doing the collecting. Then the weird feeling I was getting from Mikhail's partner, and my worries about letting him leave with her.

"You think someone is trying to pierce the Veil? Here?" Rose seemed confused by the prospect.

"I'm not sure if they are collecting to do that or for something else, but last time I witnessed someone trying to use that many, it was back in Germany during the war. Though they were going to use live people, it would have decimated half of Germany."

"You have told me bits and pieces, I know it's hard for you to remember it all." I felt my body being pulled into her. "You still carry that weight, and now there has been more added."

"The plight of living as long as I have." I sank into her pink chest. Her warm body was a comfort.

"Then let's finish this. Also, that Charlotte woman…I agree, somethings not right with that one. I didn't like how she felt this first time she walked into the cafe. Which is probably why she stayed outside earlier.Do you think Mikhail will be okay?"

"She wouldn't dare hurt him, too small a town. Too many witnesses and I have an alibi for tonight, the Sheriff wouldn't be able to pin it on me." I heard Rose laugh and hug me closer rubbing her chin on the top of my head, pushing my face down into her chest further.

If I could be smothered to death, that would be a hell of a way to go.

We turned our attention to the papers, and not too long after Rose spoke up.

"I wonder if these coordinates listed are up off that old access road on the way into town."

"What do you mean?"

"I can't remember clearly, but we were new to town back then. I remember there being a huge backup on the highway, my father got out of the car to go and see what was going on. Something about the county inspector trying to stop someone from moving equipment up a new road." I could tell she was thinking pretty hard. "I know I have driven past it heading down to Detroit. If you blink you will miss it."

"If someone took these plans with the intention of using them, they would need a way to get up into the mountain. Being away from town proper would make it much easier."

I felt a small amount of weight lift off my chest. I would have to check a map, but even if the road wasn't on the map I could figure out where the building would be. I finally had something to tell Mikhail.

"Before you get any bright ideas, you are not leaving right now. Nothing is going to change before morning, and Agent Lewis is human. He needs to sleep."

I sank back into the cushions and sighed. She had to be right didn't she.

Rose had kept me in her home until almost noon. She insisted that I needed the rest. I wanted to disagree with her but that was something she didn't allow me to do. I didn't have the fight in me.

Lucky for me, once she did release me back to the world, showered and with a new set of clothing on, I was able to quickly find a map. All the guide offices and souvenir shops had them on metal racks out front. The old map may have been more useful, but I didn't want to go back out to Sal's shop, and hope it was still in the cab of his truck.

I rode my trike to the lawn in the town center, pulling up under one of the large trees. I unfolded the cheap map, folding it once down the center to isolate the area north of the lake. Even though the map was pretty basic it did have the grid for coordinates on it. If Rose was right; the road would be taking anyone going out there, way out of the way, but it would effectively bypass many if not all hiking trails, cabins, and popular camping areas.

I began to become increasingly more eager to talk to Mikhail. Though that would mean Charlotte being around as well. That I was not excited about. Not after yesterday. I had to figure out what she knew, and who she was. I tucked the map into the bag at my hip.

I would have to just bite my tongue, share what I knew, and hope for the best. What choice did I have in the matter? I could go by myself, but that seemed like a bad idea. I didn't know what or who I would encounter up there, and I wasn't going to test it.

Taking my trike back to the street, I headed towards the motel, because I didn't see either of the agents' cars in town.

Maybe he was getting some much-needed rest. At least I hoped.

Chapter 18

Mikhail

I woke up later than I had intended this morning. I felt grog-gy. Maybe eating both of those donuts right before going to sleep had not been the best idea, or maybe it was considering I slept like a rock. Going to the bathroom I took care of my ever-bothersome scruff on my face and also realized that I should have packed more shirts. I have never been a heavy packer.

I hadn't gotten a call from the coroner's office yet, so maybe he didn't compile that file for us as quickly as he said he would. I looked at the digital clock on the nightstand of the bed. Charlotte hadn't been over to bother me either. She was usually an early riser.

I dressed in the cleanest one of my shirts, gun and badge on. Coffee was in my future. I opened my door and was startled by Charlotte holding a couple of coffees in her hands and a white bag.

"I thought you would like some coffee with your report." I noted the folder tucked up under her arm that matched the others that were in the stack on my table. I also noted that the coffee's lacked the pink sleeve around the middle of them, meaning they were not from Rose's cafe.

"You would be correct." I stepped aside to let her come in. She could apparently see the displeasure on my face as she handed me the coffee.

"I went to the little shack down by the boat launch at the lake. I went for a walk this morning. Thought it would be a nice change from the same thing you have been drinking. The man behind me in line said the crullers are better than his grandmas." I grunted and took a sip. It was acceptable. I think my standards for coffee have gotten way too high being in this town. Rose has me spoiled.

"It will do." I sat down at the table and pushed some of the files away to make room. Charlotte handed me the file and I flipped it open.

"I see you haven't opened the file I gave you last night?" Sitting down across from me, she glanced at the top of the stack on the table and shrugged.

"I was tired. It can wait." I looked at her over the open paperwork in my hand. Looking over the coroner's report, it was very much the same as the others. Though he seemed a bit lazier in his note taking than before. Maybe it didn't feel it was that important to him since Charlotte had been with him.

The newest victim was a bit older than the others, not in as good of shape. It was noted the man had a shoulder replacement. Which was different from the other victims, who had all been in peak physical condition. Maybe he wasn't involved like the other victims were. It may not be important; a man was dead.

"Do what you want. Just make sure to report to the office today, I saved your butt yesterday with them. I know you said your pager died, but there are still phones."

"I know, and I'll get a new pager when we get back."

"Miss Galloway check in with you yet? She should have gotten those blueprints by now."

"I'm sure she will call, or more likely she will show up when she finds something, that's more her style."

"That's the only reason she always seems to show up when you need her to." Sarcasm. I didn't really like the implications of her words. Her tone was not exactly what I would call friendly.

"She's just as focused on the case. Maybe you should go check in with Marcella at the library. She might not have been able to get Tailen the blueprints last night." I may have been a little too harsh with my tone, because Charlotte stood up and straightened her jacket abruptly.

"I was just thinking that wouldn't be a bad idea." She furrowed her brow and headed to the door. "Just remember we are here for a case. Letting a woman, you won't see after this dictate your next move on it, isn't like you."

The slam of the door made her point. Fucking hell. I know she is dealing with a lot, but she is usually much cooler headed.

There were some words of truth in her statement. I hadn't thought about what would come after leaving here. I guess I didn't figure that into the equation last week. Though it wasn't every day I had a gorgeous, intelligent, and unique person waltz into my life like Tailen had.

I tossed the folder onto the table and rubbed my face in frustration. I hated waiting. If I was going to sit here waiting for answers, the least could do was look at the file my partner seemed so concerned with. I grabbed it from the top of the stack and unwound the string that held it shut. Reaching in, I pulled out a small stack of papers that were all inconsistent in size. The paper felt old under my fingertips.

I tossed the envelope to the side and turned the pages upright in my hands. On the top was a worn, old photo. It looked as if it was hand developed, not like most of the pictures we had at the bureau that were done by a machine.

In the picture was a group of people lined up and dressed in uniforms that anyone with a shred of knowledge of history would recognize. The uniforms of the Nazi Party. One of the worst wars in modern history was started by them, and I was confused as to why a photo of a unit of them was sitting in my hands right now. It wasn't the best quality, but I could make out some of the faces in the group. My brow furrowed as it landed on one. A face that was next to mine not even a day ago.

Tailen Galloway.

I angrily dropped the photo onto the table and looked at the next page. It was a cutting from a German newspaper, worn from age, stapled to a blank white sheet to stabilize it. I couldn't read the words on the page, as they were foreign to me, but a translation was typed on the next page. I could feel my leg starting to shake as the anger rose in my chest. The translation spoke of a group that was doing experiments to further the Fuhrer's power though science, that would change the tide of the war in their favor. That their scientists were making breakthroughs to make their soldiers stronger. What the fuck was I reading?

Another picture slipped from between the pages. It landed on top of the other one. It was a close up of three people. A man flanked by two women, still in their uniforms, but without their hats. One of them was Tailen. Her face was serious. Her hair was lighter in the picture, pulled back into a tight bun.

I threw the pictures on the table. I stood up and resisted the urge to flip the table itself over, rubbing my head with my hands. What did the department want me to do with this? I was having trouble compiling my thoughts. This had nothing to do with the case. Why would Charlotte bring this to me? Did she know this whole time? Why not just tell me when she arrived that she knew about this? Why did it even matter?

What did it even mean? I sat down hard on the bed, growling loudly. I knew she was old, but a literal Nazi? Was that why she was in this podunk little town? Hiding out from retribution? It wasn't out of the question; others had fled to South America after the war. This, this was a lot. I had a case to think about. It was high time that I got my head on straight about it. That was the problem now. Not only had I found out that the woman I wanted to be close to was not human, but that she was part of some of the most horrible experiments in human history. Could I even trust that she wasn't just hiding details of the case from me. Maybe she wasn't as innocent in all this as she seemed.

My head was starting to hurt. It was too much.

A knock at my door made me realize that I had been sitting in my own anger for longer than I thought.

"It's open." I shouted, louder than I needed. Anger still swimming around in my brain. I looked up as the door opened, thinking that it was going to be Charlotte. It was not. It was the last person I wanted to see.

Tailen. Beautiful as ever. Though in my anger I couldn't see that right now.

"Mikhail, I got the blueprints. They had coordinates..." She stopped short as she came in the door. Her head cocking to one side. "What's wrong? Are you okay? Did something happen?"

"I would say so Miss Galloway." I tried to keep my voice down, because if I didn't, I was going to yell. "Shut the door."

"What happened?" The door closed behind her, she took a few steps towards me, but I put a hand up to stop her from moving closer to me. I hung my head down and gestured towards the table.

"You tell me." I gritted my teeth. It was hard enough having to deal with a case that was making me work outside of my expertise, and a partner who was being anything but helpful since she arrived. These photos were pushing me to my limit.

"What?" She turned to the table; her eyes grew and her face flushed red. I could see the anger rising on her own face as she snatched the photos up in her hand. Her voice was shaking, not with confusion, but with anger. She shook the papers in her hands, the edges of them crumpling and tearing. "Where did you get these? Where?"

"I don't think you are the one who should be asking questions. I think you should be the one providing answers as to why you are decked out in the uniform of Germany's finest fuck up."

"You want answers? I want to know how you got photos that were destroyed. They shouldn't exist."

"Really, that's your response to me finding out you're a fucking Nazi? That I shouldn't know? When were you going to tell me then? After the next time I let you seduce me?"

"Seduce you? I remember you being a willing participant. You do not get to send accusations flying my way when you have no idea what these photos even are."

"Then enlighten me." I rose off the bed. The tension in the room was growing. I stood up and squared my body to hers. "Though I'm not sure what an acceptable explanation for this is."

I could see her eyes turning black. They pierced right through me, her face and ears getting redder by the second. Internally I wondered if it was a good idea to square off with someone who could kill me without even thinking about it.

"It was complicated. There were so many lives at stake, I had no choice but to join them. I'm going to ask you again;

how did you get these pictures Mikhail?" Her shaking hands tearing holes into the papers, at a glance I could see her ever sharpening nails digging into the flesh of her hand.

"Head office sent them down with Charlotte. They apparently wanted me to know who I was working with. Which, at this point I'm glad for. Now I can finish this case without any distraction." I watched the anger leave her face, replaced with complete hurt.

"I don't know how she got these. That woman is not to be trusted. There is no way your government had these pictures Mikhail. I destroyed that place down to its last fucking brick. There was not a soul alive when I walked away from that rubble." Her voice was low. Her eyes left me and looked back to the pictures grimacing. "I lost a piece of myself in that place. I thought that after sleeping for so long I would wake up, and it would all be over."

"What are you even talking about?" She shoved the paper at me, knocking me back a few steps. I had to brace myself on the wall to not fall over. Tailen's hands dropped to her sides.

"She knows about it. So apparently, I didn't do a good enough job. The past is coming back to haunt me. I thought I would have outlived it." I watched her eyes glass over, if that was even possible for her.

"Fuck. Just fucking tell me." I paced away from her again. Throwing the pictures on the bed. Sitting down hard once more on its edge. "If you want me to trust anything that comes out of your mouth again and not compromise all the work done on this case." I felt defeated. Conflicted. Hurt.

Tailen slipped her bag over her head, letting it fall to the floor. Her hand pulling up the side of her shirt and off over her head as she turned to her side. This was not the time to be taking off clothing, and I would normally not complain.

"There are not many things on this side of the veil that can hurt me. Let alone kill me or leave permanent damage. This scar..." She shivered." This scar is the only thing that I thought was left of my time spent in that cesspool they called a lab." Her hand went over the scar on her side. It was larger than I could remember it being. As if a huge chunk of flesh had been taken out of her side and then healed over though not well. It didn't however disrupt the sigil tattoos that were now fading in on her skin. I looked away from her down to the floor.

"What were you doing there?" I clenched my fingers into my thighs.

"I had gotten wind during the start of the war that there was a group who was doing experiments on non-humans, and I was traveling with my partner at the time. I couldn't turn a blind eye to those sorts of rumors. She wanted to go with me, even at my protests, but we were able to use some of her medical skills to get ourselves into Germany. Pretending to be nurses who were interested in helping during the war effort. When we got close to the town where the lab was, my brother...was there to greet us."

"Wait, Brother? You have a brother."

"Had, He is the man in the picture. The other woman was my partner, her name is...was Francis. Once we were close to the town, they had their lab in, I could feel him. Which meant he knew I was there. It was almost immediate that he came to me before we could even find a place to bed down for the night. He wanted me to join him. More than threatened to kill Francis if I didn't. In his mind, there was no way that I should refuse him. I didn't want to join in the atrocities he was doing, but I needed to be close to him."

Tailen leaned herself against the wall. Her arms going around her middle head leaning back on the wall. This was not something she liked talking about. I can understand not wanting to talk about trauma, but I needed to know, I needed to be able to trust her.

"So, you're telling me you joined up with the Third Reich to stop experiments on a rumor?"

"I felt at the time I had little choice. I was right. He wasn't doing experiments to enhance humans. The experiments were a cover for his real intentions. My brethren for as long as I can remember have been trying to rip through to this side of The Veil. They feel as if it is their right. They feel slighted that The Veil has been closed. That maybe if they rip enough of the world apart that they will get the attention of those who closed it off in the first place. They were no mere experiments. He had found a ritual, pieces and texts that had been thought lost to time and was gathering the pieces to perform it. It would have taken a lot of energy to power the incantation. The sacrifice it would have taken for the ritual to work would have been immense. So, before he could wipe out half of Germany, I killed him. Do you understand how hard it is to rip my kind from existence?"

She slid down to the floor. Her long black hair covered her body as she hung her head. I was unsure of what to say. I couldn't quite process what she was saying, I had to continue to ask questions or else I would just sit here confused.

"The Germans could have claimed an atomic bomb hit them." Her head raised, her face appearing through the wall of hair, and she nodded.

"That was his plan. It would continue the war further, creating more death, more chaos and my brethren on the other side would have been able to join us. Create further chaos. We were once worshiped as Gods, well they were. I do not hold such things in myself. They despise humanity and blame it for their eternity spent beyond the veil. As if it is humans' fault. As if the creators did abandon us. I had to stop him. I had to kill one of my kind to keep that from happening. I had to erase my brother to end it. I had to literally sink my teeth and claws into one of my kind and eat his soul. Then, I had to destroy it all. One thing the Nazi's were good at was covering their mistakes. When it was found that the lab and all its off sites were being razed to the ground, it was like they never existed in the first place. Wiped from history, like most of humanity's great failures."

The thought of seemingly such a small woman ripping her way through Germany during the war, would make me question the sanity of someone telling me the story. I had to remember that if she wanted to rip me apart to hide the truth, she could.

"So that's why the history books don't have anything to say about it. Granted, I'm not sure that Hitler has shaken the rumors of dabbling in supernatural to win the war."

"The history books seem to omit most things that non-humans do. Humans still like to forget that we are here. Act like we don't exist. Even though I am not the only one to have sacrificed for them. Even Francis...one of their own, will never be remembered as a hero. She saved them just as much as I did. History will never even know her name. She is part of the reason I have tried to just live quietly."

I couldn't take her sitting on the floor alone anymore. I stood up and ripped the blanket from the bed. I walked over and placed it around her and slid down next to her on the floor. I could never understand that sort of weight.

"I will not say that I understand, but that would be a rather huge lie to cover up a couple of old photos. Considering you could kill me without any effort, I don't have any choice but to take your word on it." I shifted my legs to be out in front of me, leaning back on the wall. She clutched the blanket around her tighter. I have never been good with words of comfort.

"I wouldn't kill you, or anyone else if I didn't have to. I just don't know where those would have come from. I must have missed something or someone. I was so tired, weak. I slept for so long."

"I'll call the office, they may know where Charlotte got the file if she got it from them."

"I never told anyone about what I did. I woke up about five years ago. I haven't even told Sal or Rose about it. They know I was there, but no details. I don't want to burden them with it." I wrapped my arm over her shoulders, pulling on her. Her body fell against mine with little effort. I was always surprised that such a small frame could weigh as much as she did. I put my other arm around her and put my head on top of hers.

I felt the weight sink into my chest. What was the goal of Charlotte giving me that file, unless she wanted to create a rift between myself and Tailen. Make me question everything she has told me during the case. The question is why my partner would do that. It made little sense to me.

I needed to find out where she got those pictures. Why did she want Tailen away from me?

I was finding it hard to ask her to move so I could reach the phone. For the moment I would just let her lay on me. It seemed like she needed to. Though I didn't like the circumstances, it was nice to see her in her more natural state. Her long hair, and heavily tattooed skin. The wisps of shadow scrawling along her flesh. A reminder that she was different, and beautiful.

If only the phone was not on the nightstand.

Chapter 19

Tailen

I haven't felt this stressed in a long time. Not even in the factory when I thought Mikhail was going to get killed. The pressure in my chest, my racing heart, was worse than when I first woke up from my long slumber.

Laying against Mikhail was making the thoughts easier. Helping the stress subside. I didn't like thinking about those days, all the death and destruction. When I woke up, I wanted to get away from it. I wanted to feel the way I did before the war. More human. I felt Mikhail shift, and when I turned my eyes up, he was looking towards the phone

"You should make that call." I pushed myself away from him and sat up on my own. He patted my shoulder as he slid away from me and went to the phone.

I looked at my shirt laying on the floor. I really had to make a point didn't I. I took a deep breath in and stood up from the floor. I ran my hands back through my hair and twisted it around my hand. Then twisted that around into a bun at the back of my head. Luckily it was thick enough to stay put for the time being. Grabbing my shirt from the floor I pulled it over my head to cover my bare chest back up.

I could hear Mikhail's side of the phone conversation now that I was paying attention. He didn't sound pleased. His brow was furrowed hard, free hand clenching into a fist.

"What do you mean that Charlotte was going back to her mother's? She was literally just here this morning. I need you to go check her apartment. YES NOW." His voice raised at the end, and he slammed the receiver back to the phone.

"What happened..."

"They didn't send any files, because Charlotte was never sent. Her mother had to go back to the hospital, so she called to let them know she wouldn't be in." He strode across the room, his hand on his gun. "No wonder she was acting weird. I thought it was just stress. I should have known."

Mikhail walked past me, flinging the room door open and took off out of the building. I followed quickly behind him. The car she had driven in still sat in the parking lot in front of the room. Mikhail had one hand still on his gun, his other beat on the door of one of the rooms.

"Charlotte. Open the door. OPEN THE DOOR." His voice was full of anger. I came up next to him. There was no sound of movement in the room. I pushed the door hard with my hand. It sprung open, the sound of cracking wood as the hinges pulled from the door frame.

The room was dark, it looked freshly made. Nothing had been moved since the last time it was cleaned. No luggage, no trash, nothing. As if no one had stayed in it at all. Mikhail stood in the middle of the room and growled loudly.

"It wasn't her Tailen. How fucking stupid am I? I should have noticed it wasn't her. I just thought that she was on edge because of her mom. When she didn't make the joke she usually does about our last names...when she made comment about my sexuality..."

"This explains why she knew about my scar. She told me that it always hurts more when it's family. I knew something was off, but I didn't know that wasn't how your partner usually behaved." He shook his head and stormed out past me.

"That's her car. I swear if she is hurt." He hit the hood of the sedan with the side of his fists and turned around leaning on the hood, rubbing his face.

"If she was trying to wedge us apart. It's because we are closing in on something with this case, and she doesn't want us to know. It doesn't make sense in pieces but together...."

"You think that the spirit attacks, someone impersonating my partner, and whatever you went to look for at the cemetery is connected? That's a lot of pieces. Also, she targeted you. Why?"

"I must assume that I am a wrench in the plans. A normal FBI agent, a few murders in a tourist town with spirits, would have been done and over with quickly. Possibly unsolved fully." Not that I wanted to take credit away from him, but it couldn't be a coincidence that she used those photographs that she would not have easily been able to obtain to try and dissolve the faith he put in me.

"She knew you though, and what exactly did you find at the cemetery?"

"That's part of what I came to tell you. There was a sigil there, a big one. It's one that could possibly be used to trap and collect spirits resting there."

"Power. It's not about five dead people. It's about every deceased person in town. You said that the iron keeps them here, that it's hard for them to leave." I could see the wheels turning for him, like they did me.

"If they collected and stored enough somehow, then it could be used to do serious damage to this town. Which is why I think that company bought all those mining properties."

"All those people that died in the mine collapse. They wanted to know where to dig a new shaft, so they could get down there."

The pieces were starting to fit together a little better. The victims had just been workers. They were either killed while working, or because they were in the way. The greed for power was coming full circle almost 30 years later. I followed Mikhail back towards his own room. His stride was long and heavy.

We didn't have time to waste. I grabbed my bag from the floor and pulled out the papers that Marcella had given me, along with the cheap map I had gotten from the souvenir stand. I pointed out the coordinates to him.

"Rose says that she remembers there being an access road off the highway. Do you remember seeing anything when you drove in?"

"Can't say that I did, but I wasn't really paying attention. When I was driving up, I was more interested in getting this case over with. I honestly didn't think that the deaths would be connected at all at first. I figured it was just animal attacks or the like." I couldn't blame him, not exactly a fun case to take on mostly alone, with a mildly inept Sheriff spouting nonsense the moment he walked into the station.

Mikhail was headed to the door, and I was on his heels, bag and map in tow. I wanted to go into this prepared. I would not have a repeat of the last time. I also did not want to involve my friends. Sal, Rose, and Marcella had already done more for us than I could ask for.

"We have to be prepared, Mikhail. No mistakes like last time. We must stop by my cabin. We can take the cut through the woods back to the highway." He grunted but conceded. I could tell that he was itching to get this over with, just like I was.

The tires of the SUV crunched on the gravel as Mikhail kicked it into reverse. He took off at high speed through town. Luckily with the sun setting the streets were mostly clear, tourists having settled into their cabins and by campfires for the night. I could make out the lights in Rose's apartment. I hoped that her night would be more comfortable than mine.

The familiar trees of my home came into view. Mikhail pulled up faster than I would have liked and stopped short of the stairs. What we needed was under the house in my workshop. I jumped out leaving the door open. I heard Mikhail's footsteps behind me.

"Salt, and dried Heilige." I said albeit to myself. Pushing aside the curtain that covered my shelving. I had almost forgotten about the deer hanging in the workshop. It admittedly didn't smell great. Grabbing on the bottom shelf I took a burlap bag, full of salt and turned around handing it to Mikhail, who seemed surprised by the weight.

"What are those?" His eyes ran over the shelving, the topmost were filled with pots. In them grew small purple and green plants, they were leafy, and resembled ferns. I took a bundle that hung on the end of one of the shelves.

"Heilige. It's a plant that grows where the Veil is thin. It seems that it also likes to grow around me. It has various uses. Not for humans thought. So don't eat it." I grabbed an empty jar. I could mix on the way.

"Noted. Don't eat the weird plant." He continued to eye it warily.

"I don't have any firearms like Sal, hopefully we won't need that, but I do have this." I walked to my work bench and grabbed a long knife from the wall above it. "It's cold forged iron. Should be at least enough, and Spirits do not like to get close to it. Skins deer quite well for how old it is."

"How old is it?" Mikhail turned the knife over in his hand after I handed it to him. Admiring the sharp blade and the simple handle.

"Older than you. I think that's all. Do you think we need anything else?" He shook his head, and we went back to the running waiting vehicle.

As we drove, I crunched the dried plant, and salt down into the glass jar. Stopping briefly to get Mikhail on the right road that would take us back towards the highway into town.

The road was dirt, but named, had a couple of cabins off it. I grabbed a handful of the leaves of the plant and dropped them on top of the mixture in the jar and then lit them with the cigarette lighter from the SUVs console. They began to smolder, and I twisted the metal lid back on.

"That's different than before...." Mikhail glanced briefly over, but kept his focus mostly on the road, as we came out onto the state highway. He checked the mile marker sign we passed to make sure we were headed the right direction.

"Better protective circle than just salt. Like I said, be prepared. I would rather you not have a matching scar on your other side." I watched the road, the glint of a fence coming into view between the trees, and the headlights of the car hitting some skid marks on the road. They looked bigger than regular car tire tracks, it seems Mikhail saw them before I did because he slowed down, and started looking for the turn off.

The road that Mikhail turned off onto was dirt, and it would have been almost invisible had the bushes and brush not been crushed and dragged away from a now opened yet rusted cattle gate. The Do Not Enter sign was hanging on by a zip tie, and looked as if it would fall off if the wind blew wrong. It was apparent that large vehicles had been through here at least semi-recently. Broken branches of trees, smushed up bushes that once grew over the old access road. Mikhail drove as quickly as he could, but the woods grew a bit thicker. It felt like we were so far away from town.

After a couple of miles, the road opened up, and piles of dirt and rock began to appear on the sides of the road. Getting gradually bigger as we drove.

"They look fresh. It looks like they have been digging. I guess you were right about that new shaft." His hands tightened and twisted on the wheel. I reached over and placed my hand on his arm. His eyes didn't leave the road.

"This would have taken weeks, if not longer. They relied on the fact tourist season would have everyone so focused on the lake, the police more concerned with petty crime in town, than noise or activity across the water. Plus no one comes out to the far side banks, not more than a hiker or two anyway."

"Remind me later to pick your brain on good detective work. You put some of our best to shame, you know that."

"As long as I have been alive, you just learn how humans behave. I don't know everything, and humanity still surprises me after all this time, however those officers in town, they don't go out of their way." Mikhail laughed and shook his head.

"That's for damn sure."

The road opened up, we passed by old mining equipment, rusted by the passage of time and the elements beating on them for a couple decades. The ruins seemed almost calm in the waning sun skipping off the derelict cranes and drills. Turned over bulldozers with their scoops still in piles of iron and dirt, overgrown by plant life. We passed by a collapsed shaft with worn signage painted over the wood of the old entrance.

Our car came to a halt. I could see the shine of a new dump truck filled with dirt. We had found our new dig site. The truck didn't seem to have any sort of company branding.

"We should go on foot. If anyone is up here, they may already have heard us drive up." He stepped out of the door. I heard him check his gun before returning it to his holster. Then reached back in to grab the knife I had given him. We met each other in front of the vehicle.

The sounds of the night were distant. An owl flew overhead, the beating of its wings were the only animal noise I had heard in miles. I shrugged my bag tighter on my shoulder. The weight of the jar tucked inside felt heavy for some reason.

"One thing before we head up." I turned my face towards him and was met by his lips. It was sudden, and rough. The surprise on my face when he pulled away caused him to chuckle. "I needed reassurance. I'm sorry."

"Don't apologize." The unexpected affection was comforting.

I cleared my throat as we moved past the new truck. We had to get this solved. I didn't want that to be the last time I felt his lips on mine. He always tasted like coffee.

More mining equipment came into view. Recently used. There was no movement in any of the equipment. I could see lights coming into view. The sound of a generator humming away could be heard. As we rounded a pile of rubble I could see the entrance of the new mining shaft.

"Shouldn't there be people…this is a big operation." His voice was suspicious.

"You would be right. Even if they sent people home for the night or weekend, an operation like this would at least have a night guard." I closed my eyes. I couldn't feel the presence of anything other than Mikhail stuck to my side.

"Maybe they didn't think anyone would come out this way. They have been operating for a while with no issue…." His eyes scanned the scene hand on his gun, flipping the knife over in his free hand.

"I know you are not going to like this, but you should let me go in first. Let me set up protection. If there is a spirit down there, I don't want a repeat." He furrowed his brow at me and took a deep breath.

"Unfortunately, I have to agree. I know that you are the last person I need to worry about. I can watch the entrance, make sure that we are not missing someone." I breathed a sigh of relief. It made me feel much better that he would be out of harm's way. Well, the potential harm. At least for now.

I let my hand touch his arm as I walked away from him and entered the tunnel that led down into the earth.

It was heavily reinforced with steel. Much better than mine shafts would have been back in the sixties. A line of dimly lit metal caged lamps hung on hooks connected by thick wires. Rocks crunched under my feet, the shadows around them grew. I felt myself spreading out through the shadows of the shaft. The slow shallow grade of the slope was meant for ease of removing debris. An abandoned mining cart pushed against one of the walls was still filled with freshly dug rock.

The chamber at the bottom of the slope expanded, the lights fanning out along the walls, wires coming from another generator to power large halogen lamps on stands. Lighting up the room. It was the smell that caused me to be off guard, my shadowed tendrils retreating to my skin. Off to one side I could see an opening leading to another darkened chamber. I stopped towards the center of the room. There were signs in the dirt of recent activity. The equipment that was in the room looked used and as if it had just been turned off not too long before we arrived.

I grabbed the jar from my bag, and turning in a circle created an unbroken line around myself. Stepping back over it, and putting the jar back into my bag, hopefully that would be enough for Mikhail should he need it. My attention was now turned to the room off to the side. They really had been doing work here, a lot of work. It looked like it hadn't stopped that long ago.

As I approached the opening to the side chamber, I could see blood smeared on the stone of the walls. The smell of blood and decay was getting stronger. It was getting to be overwhelming. The room was even dimmer than its counterpart. The dirt beneath my feet started to darken, the soil beginning to squish instead of shift.

Blood.

There were bodies piled along the outside of the large room and were numerous. I now knew where the crew that had been digging went. It was like they had been killed mid-dig. I knelt by one of the bodies towards the center of the room. There was no sign of a spirit having killed this man, and as pushed him over onto his back, his throat was slashed. Pulling away quickly from the body I stood eyes narrowing as a figure walked out from behind one of the mining drills.

"You know. I thought you would come alone. Those pictures should have been more than enough for him to leave you in the dust." The voice was familiar.

Charlotte.

At least whomever it was pretending to be her. The red light of the end of a cigarette illuminating her face. I didn't think before the tendrils from my arms shot out, dragging her by her leg into the light. She made very little noise as she hit the ground on her back. One of my shadowed tentacles gripped around her throat, pulling her up into the air.

"I will ask once. Only once. Who are you?" A smile spread across her face the cigarette falling to the floor. I didn't notice the zippo in her hand until the spark of the flint flashed. The lighter being tossed towards me and hit the soaked ground.

That was the moment that I realized it was not all blood. The flames quickly ignited spreading out around the room in a circle. The pain I felt as the flame cut off the shadow between myself and the woman who called herself Charlotte put me down to my knee. I screamed. The searing agony of having a limb cut off was almost unbearable. As I caught my breath my eyes scanned around the room, following the circle around. The flame grew low to the ground and glowed a bright blue. Where did she get Holy Oil? How could she have gotten it?

Charlotte stood and dusted herself off. Reaching in the breast pocket inside of her jacket, pulling out a new cigarette and a Wehrmacht style lighter. Lighting it and she took a long drag before speaking again. The smoke that escaped her lips was the familiar deep green color that I knew so well. She paced back and forth, her eyes watching me. She had undone her hair, and it hung freely around her face, and the dress shirt that had been done up to the throat was now laying open. The white fabric of the shirt was splattered with blood. I could see that the cuffs of her shirt were so drenched with blood that they almost looked black.

"You should know who I am. What are you going by now? Tailen Galloway?" She took another long drag. "I guess that those protection runes I dug up actually work, even against you." I rose to my feet and spit black ichor on the ground. Stepping up to the border of the circle, I could feel the heat on my face, my hair had fallen from the bun and was cascaded down my back and stuck to the sides of my face.

"What is your endgame here, trying to separate me from Mikhail? Trapping me down here? I can't say that I know anyone who would even attempt that's still alive."

"Yet, here I am. In the flesh. Though this face is new." She rubbed the side of her face, sort of pulling at her cheek. "The memories though, are old. However, they are still as fresh as the day you tore your brother apart. Tore it all apart and burned it all to the ground. To be honest I didn't even know you were here. Just a happy coincidence."

"You came to collect the dead. You found a place that would be easy, and here, in this hole in the ground, you what, think you can start his work again? Tear through? Even with every one of those spirits, it's not enough. You would need millions."

"Oh, It's not, not in the least. It's a start though. I have time. Like you do. Unlike your brother, I am a patient person. Just needed a place to test my theories." The woman leaned back on an overturned barrel. Though she had the face of a human, she was everything they were not. "When my foreman fucked up and decided dumping bodies was a good idea, I had to come and deal with the fall out. He didn't expect that a spirit would still be that strong enough to cause them problems under this mountain of iron. What I didn't expect when I got here, is that you would still be hiding behind the same face that betrayed us."

"I would do it again. Millions didn't deserve to die because my brother decided that he wanted to be a god again." I walked to the center of the circle. I was trying to make sense of all this.

"You have been getting too cozy with your humanity. Fortunately for me at this moment, I can use that to get what I want." She took another long intentional draw from the cigarette between her lips.

"I couldn't imagine why you think I would help you. Do you remember what happened to my brother? Since you apparently were there. What makes you think I would even consider helping you with anything?"

"You will give me the spirits that lie under this fallen earth. Help me dig them out, since your blood would amplify any ritual, I use it with, your agent, and your little family you have created, will not have to join the pile of bodies. Heck if I wanted, I could remove this cursed town from the map if I wanted. That would call a lot of attention, so I would rather you just do what I want so I don't have to further threaten those you seem to hold so very close."

"I know how you survived...you are a parasite."

"Fuck you. I had to survive just like you. I had no choice. I wasn't going to let you kill me. Stop our important work. You have no right..."

Not-Charolette's words cut off and her head snapped to the sounds of gunshots coming from the other chamber. The yelling of Mikhail's voice echoed against the rocks. "Looks like your little agent is about to figure out that he stepped into something he won't be able to get out of."

"Humans are not as weak as you think. Especially not that one."

Chapter 20

Mikhail

The night air gave me no comfort while I waited for Tailen to signal or come out to get me. The quiet of the drive up was just now hitting me as the sound of the wind and the generator was the only thing filling the void. I leaned on the steel beams holding up the entrance of the mine shaft. I tried to breathe deeply and keep my cool.

Out of the corner of my eye I saw movement. We hadn't seen any other activity, so it caught my attention. The shadows grew and I could now hear the sound of steps on the crunching on the loose gravel. I drew my gun and held it with the knife Tailen had gifted me.

"FBI announce yourself." I yelled, planting my feet.

The shadows did not stop coming forward. It was when they stepped into the light of the now rising moon that I realized they did not look right. Their blank glossed over white eyes. The fact that they had blood trailing down from their necks that had long since dried and stuck their t-shirts to their chests. They looked like they had been dragged through the dirt. I took a step back, gun trained on them. Their gait was labored, almost robotic in nature.

"Stop and identify yourself. I will shoot." My heart began to race. This was not good; this was not something that had been covered in any sort of training. I took another step back into the opening of the shaft and gritted my teeth. They did not stop. I had to try something even if it wasn't going to work. I fired off two shots, hitting one of the men square in his chest. Only thing it did was cause him to pause for a step and fall behind slightly.

"Fuck." I stepped down into the dim shaft. My time waiting on Tailen was over. I took off on a jog down the path into the mine. The chamber at the bottom opened up, and I looked around for anything that would give me some cover. It looked like an overturned pile of wheelbarrows was the quickest option.

I could hear the sounds of crackling, even over the generator. Was that a fire? Down here? Where was it coming from? The smell finally hit my nose. The stench of death, bile, and blood, there was more death here than just those miners that got caught during the collapse.

Looking over the wheelbarrows, I could see the shadows of the two men entering the open room. I breathed in deeply and tried to follow their movements as they came in. They both stopped. Heads turning to gaze around the room. Where was Tailen?

That's when I felt it. The cold. The creeping chill that unfortunately I had gotten used to. Why now? I had to do more than sit here and wait for something bad to happen. I stood up quietly, my weapon trained on the two men beginning to move towards the other side of the room. It was then I noticed the circle of salt in the center of the room. The site of that as I could start to see my breath was the relief I needed.

I wasn't sure if it would work on whatever those things are, but It sure as hell would go against whatever spirit I could see taking form. I quickly moved towards the center of the room. Both men turned to look at me as my feet stepped over the salt line. I knew it wasn't going to do anything, but I fired anyway.

Shooting at the two men, I got one in his head, and the velocity took him down to the ground. The other one however picked up his speed across the room towards me. I took a couple more futile shots at him.

That's when a rush of cold hit my bad shoulder, it made it ache so bad I dropped my gun into the dirt by my feet. The man who had taken a run at me was now flying across the room, his body making a horrific crunching sound as it hit the jagged mine wall.

It was like time slowed down. The figure of a woman stood before me. Looking at her in the face, I could see the lights behind her, but it was like looking through an aquarium. Her face was clearer than the specter at the factory, even more than Mrs. Bea. I could make out defined features.

She was young. Her hair was pulled up in a high ponytail, her features were European, with soft eyebrows. She was dressed in work clothing, and it didn't seem like it fit the rest of her clean-cut appearance. The one thing that struck me is she didn't look angry. She just looked at me. Her mouth opened to speak, but no words came out. I shook my head.

"I can't understand you." A look of frustration came over her face. She turned towards the man who was starting to now get back to his feet. The cold surrounding her was almost unbearable, and I was thankful when she flew away from me.

As the man stood up the specter hit him square in the chest, the shimmering light of her form disappearing into the man's torso. He convulsed for a few seconds. I looked over towards the one that had been thrown against the wall. His body was still slumped on the floor.

"They are doing...It...again." The words were breathy, as if the man was drowning while the words formed. The sound of his voice was mixed with the higher tone of a woman like they were speaking in stereo. His body stood up and moved towards me. The movements were smoother than before. "They are ...digging... again."

"I...don't understand."

"They have already been through enough. I tried to stop them but they...they keep digging." It was clear that the words were strained, that she was struggling to find the words to say. As if she was searching for the correct thing to say. Stopping short of the circle, the man's head cocked to one side. Not that I wanted to, but I could finally get a good look at the body that this spirit was inhabiting. Clearly his neck had been slashed, by something sharp enough that it left no jagged marks on the slice that went almost all the way through the neck. I could see through a jagged hole in the chest of the shirt what looked like symbols carved into the decaying flesh, it was oozing fluid. Smelled horrible.

"I'm not here to dig. I think you know that though...." I shifted on my feet and looked at the ground. It wasn't smart. I knew it wasn't but, I put my foot on the line of salt and pushed it away breaking the circle. The man's head clicked back to center.

"You are not. The woman with blonde hair...she wants...." The man's hands went to his head, as if he was trying to think hard.

"Did you see a black-haired woman? She...We can make it stop." I dropped my hands to my sides and looked across the room, I could see the flicker of flames though the doorway that was across the room.

"The fire...It hurts me. Could smell the oil through the blood..." The blank expression contorted a bit into that of pain. "Too hot."

I had to think quickly. I bent down and grabbed the gun that was sitting in the dirt near my feet. I dropped the magazine and reached to grab the extra on my belt. I needed to be calm. I hoped that my act of trust towards the spirit would be enough. I moved past the man and headed towards the opening in the rock wall that led towards the next room.

I was making more stupid choices. It was clear that Tailen was in trouble there. I took a shot into the opening, making sure it hit the ceiling. Moving forward, I could hear the scrape of steps behind me. Another shot fired into the room this time. Stopping I could hear a familiar voice.

"Do I have to do everything my fucking self." The woman I thought was Charlotte stomped her way into the light of the room. "Why are you not dead yet?"

"Can't get rid of me that easily." I trained my gun on her. I could feel the man come up beside me.

"You humans just don't know when to quit." She threw the cig from her hand down onto the floor and stamped on it with the heel of her shoe. I could see her hands extend, her nails extending and sharpening.

"Well at least I don't have to wear a face that I stole." I cocked my eyes sideways, "No offense."

All I got was a guttural grunt from the man beside me.

"What..." It was all Charlotte could get out before I heard the body next to me drop to the floor and the cold hit my body as the spirit flew at her. It must have taken her by complete surprise because she was on the floor slashing at the air. Her body lifted from the ground as the spirit took her by the neck. It apparently hurt bad from the scream she let out.

I took the opportunity to take off in a sprint towards the other room. The heat of the room was almost as unbearable as the cold from the spirit. I holstered my gun and tried to let my eyes adjust to the lighting. The low blue fire wasn't emitting much light. I could however see Tailen approaching the wall of flames.

"Mikhail! What...what happened." Her voice held panic in it.

"Later...I need to get you out." I knew better than to reach for the fire, lesson learned about putting my hands into something I didn't know. I looked around the room. "Break the circle, right?"

Tailen nodded and helped me look around the room. I could hear screeching coming from the other chamber. I had to work fast. The pile of overturned barrels seemed like the best option. Moving to them, I braced myself against a mine cart and planted my feet on the side of one of the barrels. I took some quick breaths in and pushed as hard as I could. They shifted under the pressure, breaking free of the rust that encased them. Creaking and starting to roll, I gave a firm hard kick to the same barrel and that did the trick.

The barrels rolled, not quickly but enough to pick up speed to and roll into the flames. It must have been enough because the flames died in that part of the circle, and Tailen was quick enough to jump over the opening landing hard in front of me. She reached for me, pulling me fast to my feet. Nodding quickly, she took off to the other room, and I was on her heels.

There was no sign of the blonde woman, nor the spirit who had turned the tide of the fight. Tailen stopped only briefly before taking off up the entrance slope.

I stopped to breathe. Looking around the room, it seemed calm now. That's how it always was. My heart was still racing. The two bodies of the men laid still on the dirt, motionless.

The cool air flooded back in; I turned to see the spirit of the woman standing a few feet from me. She looked pleased with herself if you could call it that.

"Thank you." It was all I could say to her. She didn't move from her spot. Her eyes scanned the room around me. I could see shadows on the floor starting to rise, and fear flashed across the woman's face. I swung around and put my hands up. "No no no no wait."

"Wait?" Confusion in her voice spread across her pale face, but she looked over my shoulder at the spirit who stood still, watching the living decide her fate yet again.

"Tailen, she ran Charlotte...that woman off. She hasn't done anything wrong."

"She has probably been the one killing those men."

"I think...she was just protecting the dead miners." I held my hands up towards her.

The Shadows on the floor retreated, I could see the tendrils reforming on Tailen's skin. She took in a jagged breath and moved past me. Putting herself between me and the shimmering specter. Her hair was tangled and wild, sticking to the skin of her back and legs.

"Do you have awareness?" The woman nodded and bent down to the dirt. Her finger dragging through the dirt. Spelling a name in the soil.

Liandra.

"Wait. That's the name of Niesbieths daughter. Right?" Mikhail recalled the documents we had examined over the last week. I couldn't believe it. She was still here? After all this time. Trapped in the grave her own father made for her.

"You tried to protect them back then too, didn't you?" Tailen had softened her tone. Liandra nodded her head. Looking a bit forlorn.

"You have been protecting them long enough Liandra. You can rest. We will make sure no one comes back here."

"We can try at least. You shouldn't have to bear this burden that you have given yourself...but you are not ready to move on, are you?" The spirit shook her head again. Tailen looked down at her feet and then looked back at me.

"What can we do? I really don't know." It was the truth. Guns, detective work, running into problems, those were my forte. Helping a spirit find rest, was not.

"I will need to do research. For now, I can put protections up. I have a feeling our Not-Charlotte won't be returning. She, like me, has time and patience. Or so she told me. Whatever she is working on, it isn't worth being torn apart before she accomplishes it." She turned back to Liandra. "We will return to help. Can you wait just a little longer?"

Liandra stepped back a few steps and nodded her head. Her body dissipated, the chill in the air fell away. It was like she had never been there. The mine seemed calmer now.

Tailen breathed a sigh of relief. It was in her quietness I realized that she was hurt. It didn't look physical on the outside, but I could see the pain spreading across her face as the heat of the fight wore off. I grabbed her shoulders to steady her.

"It has been a long time since I felt this kind of pain." Her body weight sunk into me, and I planted my feet to catch it. I swung one of her arms over my good shoulder and put the knife she had given me in my belt.

We walked from that dim hole in the ground outside. The wind of the night air felt so good on my sweating skin. Tailen pushed away from me and faced the entrance.

I watched as she squared up to it. I saw her run a fingernail across the palm of her hand. Black liquid dripped from it, and she placed it on the steel beams. I wasn't sure what to make of the symbols she drew with the black blood that she was smearing but I hoped it was the protection she promised Liandra. Which seemed to be the case. As she murmured under her breath the shadows engulfed the entrance and retreated just as fast. The blood sinking into the steel. I took that as a sign that it worked.

"I really need a shower Mikhail...." She returned to my side and leaned against me again.

We were on the move down the dirt road. Tailen lay against the door, her eyes half closed, watching the trees go by. I tried to focus on my breathing, putting the events in order, making sense of everything. It played out in my mind slowly.

It felt like we were down there forever, the moon hanging high in the night sky.

I could see the lights of town, the blue neon of the motel sign looked strangely comforting. The thought of a hot shower was enough to make me forget about how hungry I actually was. I pulled in front of my room.

Stepping out of the car I went around to Tailen's side and took her arm again as she slid from the seat to her feet. I let the door fall shut and walked with her into the room.

I let her sit down on the bed. Moving away I removed my belt. Letting my gun, badge, and the knife fall to the floor, and I kicked it over by my bag. My eyes fell over Tailen who looked exhausted. Who in turn looked towards the bathroom.

"You should take that shower. Do you want help?" She shook her head and leaned down untying her boots and pushing them off her feet.

"I feel like you have calls to make. I hope your real partner is doing okay." She stood up, her fingers ran around my arm and squeezed it. She was right, I did have at least one call to make. I needed to check in, and hope that the Charlotte was in fact alive and well. Though in this moment, I wanted to make sure Tailen was okay, she was so collected.

I sat down on the armchair and grabbed the phone. I watched Tailen go into the bathroom, but even though the door wasn't shut I couldn't see her once I heard the shower turn on.

I dialed the number I knew by heart. The other end was picked up quickly. The agent on the other side sounded tired but his tone changed when I identified myself.

Charlotte was okay. That was the first thing he said. They found her in her apartment worse for wear, but alive. They got her to the hospital, and she was stable, resting. All she could remember from the attack was that the person who attacked her looked exactly like her. That she felt like she meant to kill her, but when she took a swing at the assailant stabbing them with a fork, they took off. She did end up with a few serious wounds but was alive and doing well. I was relieved that she was now taken care of.

I had them take a brief report, but I told them that they would need to send up a team to start processing the mines, and that sending the director up to deal with the Sheriff would be wise. Also, to send the Unknowns department a heads up, we were going to be needing them after the fact. Cleanup was going to have to happen. Maybe we could do something better for those trapped underneath the mountain as well as those bodies that were in the secondary chamber.

I could hear the water hitting the tile and steam filtered out into the room. Just hoped she didn't plan on using all the hot water. A shower and wrapping my arms around Tailen's waist was all I really wanted.

The stale bag of crullers on the table did however call my name.

Chapter 21

Tailen

In my hundreds of years, I had rarely encountered a spirit who could not only manifest itself but could communicate. Even Harold over at the cemetery wasn't able to do that. He just complained in a loop that could be briefly interrupted and Bea that was at the library just went about her business without regard to anyone around her. This one though, Liandra, she was something else. There would be a lot of work ahead of me to make sure that it was properly taken care of, I wasn't going to let her must stay guarding that place for eternity.

Not-Charlotte had said she had time, and as I sat on the wet tile of the shower in Mikhail's motel room, still wondering what she meant by that. She wasn't human for sure and seemed to despise them. I was angry with myself for allowing her to escape, but I couldn't leave Mikhail with what I thought was a hostile spirit alone. There were too many questions that I needed answered, but we had the ones we needed for now. That at least had lifted some weight off my shoulders.

As I leaned against the side wall, letting the water rush over me, my hair stuck to my body as the dirt and stench of death and decay washed down the drain.

"I could handle washing your hair for you if you want?" Mikhail leaned on the door jamb of the bathroom; I could hear the sound of a stale cruller being eaten.

"This is way too much for you to manage." I pushed off the floor, standing and letting the last of the soap I had scrubbed myself with rinse off. "How is she?"

"Charlotte is going to be fine. They got her to the hospital. She is a strong woman. Said her assailant took off after being stabbed by a fork?"

"If it was antique, it was probably silver. I bet she did more damage than she realized."

"I thought silver was for werewolves..."

"Lots of things don't like silver. Demons, some Fae, Changelings, Wraiths ...even some Vampires don't like it m uch..." My voice trailed off. "Well, I bet I know what attacked your partner."

"Guessing one of those things? Didn't I say I was done learning things? I feel like I am learning things."

"Changeling, or Shifter, hard to prove that though. We only know one face they used, and they have some sort of protection that made it hard for me or even Rose to pick them out as not human." I mused out loud. Wringing the ends of my hair out as I stepped to the back of the shower.

"That is a problem for another day, right now… I need to use that shower you are hogging." Mikhail dusted off his hands. His eyes trailing from mine down my wet body it was like he just now realized that I was naked. I put my hand out for him to hand me a towel. Which I then dried myself with as I stepped over the short tile edge of the shower. I pushed past him, smiling softly.

"It's all yours. Should be plenty of hot water left." He started to undress in the doorway of the bathroom. I flopped my hair to the side, drying it with the towel as I watched his pants fall to the ground, and him kick his clothing into a pile. It took a lot of effort on my part not to just go grab a handful of his butt cheeks.

I heard him yelp a bit as he got under the water, I had it turned all the way up to eleven. I laughed as I took his spot leaning on the doorway, still drying my hair.

"You could have warned me it was as hot as that blue fire in here… nearly burned off my hair."

"It's a good thing you didn't touch it. Me, it will just hurt, you…immolated. Holy Fire."

"Holy what? Like biblical?" I watched him lather up eyes trailing down his back. His skin turning pink from the heat of the shower. He looked so very tempting. The want to run my fingers up the scars on his back, around the creases of his muscles was strong.

"Not exactly. Its distilled oil made from grinding up feathers from an angel's wings. There are not many angels left, it has been about eighty years since I have seen one, so I would imagine it's hard to come by. It's one of the only things that burns hot enough to hurt me."

"Hurt you, is that why you…"

"Look tired? Yes, she took off one of my limbs with it. It will grow back in time; the pain is already subsiding."

"That was not what I was going to say." I chuckled at him trying to save a bit of face. I shook my head and leaned against the door continuing to towel off my hair.

"It's alright, I should have been more careful. I seem to have lost my touch after being asleep for so long."

"Hand me a towel?" Mikhail turned the water off and reached out towards me. I tossed my own towel over the sink and took a clean one holding it out for him. I was a little too late to react to the twinge of a smile that crossed Mikhail's lips as he pulled the towel, lurching me forward so he could grab my wrist and pull me towards him. I gasped as he pushed my body against the warm tile of the back wall of the shower. He gently leaned his body against mine and kissed me. His slick chest pushing against mine made the weight of the day fall from my mind.

I could feel his hands sliding up my sides, fingers squeezing at my hips as his tongue slid between my lips to tangle with my own. I wrapped my arms around his shoulders, running my fingers up into his hair. I groaned as he pulled away from me, leaning his forehead on mine.

"Sorry, had to take the chance while your guard was down." His hands gripped the flesh of my hips, I don't think I could tire of how his fingers felt digging into my skin.

"You know you shouldn't really surprise and corner an injured leviathan. For being an agent, you make some pretty risky decisions." I let up my grip on his hair, letting my arms drape over his shoulders loosely.

"I take calculated risks. Ones that I am willing to deal with the consequences of." His hands slid up my sides, pushing my arms up over my head, pinning my wrists above my head. His lips falling to my neck, I tilted my head to the side in response. Allowing his warm lips to send jolts of pleasure through me. I was slowly forgetting how tired I was. His tongue dragged from my shoulder all the way up to my ear, nipping at the crest. His warm breath causing me to shiver. This man had figured out in a very short time how to push my buttons.

"I really hope you mean that, because I have to let you know..." I leaned in breathing my words into his ear. "Even injured, I have more limbs than you do."

The gasp that exploded from Mikhail's lips was like music to my ears. I twisted the tentacle-like shadows that had been snaking up his legs around the hardening length of his cock. Squeezing his member tightly and twisting the tendrils around him. I felt his body twitch and his head fell against my shoulder, his hands bracing himself on the wall, dropping my wrists. I couldn't help but smirk and pull him close into me so I could feel his length on my stomach. His stiff cock twitched under my strokes, his groans and guttural moans echoed in the tiled room.

"Fuck Tal..." He finally could form words, his head lifting from my shoulder, to look at me with half lidded eyes. "I didn't know you...you could...fuck...do that." His words were strained and came out between moans. I could feel the tension in his chest as it pressed against mine. His arms flexing. It was so satisfying to feel this man pressed into me, panting as I stroked him the tendrils of shadow trailing around his thighs.

Mikhail pushed off the wall, and it seemed to take more effort than it should have. His eyes still half open, his lips parted, panting. His lips assaulted mine, hard, full of need. I couldn't deny the want I also had, the heat of my arousal slick between my legs. I wouldn't be left wanting for long.

Mikhail, through his panting, dropped to his knees before me. His mouth easily finding my center. Lifting my leg to rest on his shoulder so he could bury is face into my wet and wanting pussy. I steadied myself against the wall, nails curling into the tile, trying not to dig into hard and crack it. Fuck his tongue felt amazing. Leaning my head back into the tiles, my hips having a mind of their own, grinding into his face. His groans only got more intense as we both stroked each other towards climax.

Mikhail sucked my clit between his lips, three fingers pressing up into my slit. Sliding in and making me buck my hips. I was so fucking close to the edge. He pulled away, and I glanced down...panting. He was also close but couldn't seem to form the words.

With another couple of thrusts, I was undone. Groaning his name, my walls gripping around his fingers as he tried to pump into me though my orgasm. His hot cum hitting the inner side of my thighs. My tendrils of shadow milking every drop out of this moaning human man kneeling at my feet.

Both of us were shaking through the aftershocks, his forehead slumped forward against the tiles, letting my leg fall off his shoulder. My chest heaving as I felt the random waves of pleasure shooting through my legs and stomach. I shakily stroked though his hair. The tendrils releasing his cock and thighs.

He must have taken the release as a sign, because I felt
myself being lifted off my feet, my back leaving the cooling
tiles of the shower. Mikhail had thrown me over his shoulder
and was walking towards the bed as fast as he could.

I was surprised that the bed did not break under my weight
of my body being tossed down on it. It did crack loudly.
Mikhail's hungry eyes looked down over my form. His chest
heaving. He was so enticing, the trail of hair from his pecs
that trialed down into a line that ended at his groin. The
huge scar that covered most of his one leg, that fanned
out into his lower stomach. His blue piercing eyes hungrily
looking over my body, like he wanted to devour me.

"You are so beautiful." I almost didn't hear him. His words
were breathy, between the heaves of his chest. He pushed
himself between my knees, pushing them aside with his
own. His hands sliding up my stomach, gripping both of my
breasts flicking my nipples with his thumbs. He fell forward
lips once again crashing into mine. This kind of connection
was the thing I needed and the way that his fingers gripped
my hair, pulling me into him, told me he needed it too.

I wrapped my arms around his back, the tendrils of shadow
following and gripping him closer to me. His kisses moving
to my neck and shoulders, leaving me panting in their wake.
The murmurs of moans coming from him between the nips
and licks. All I could do was shiver at his touch, push my

hips up into his, almost desperate to feel him inside of me again.

Mikhail didn't make me wait long. He pushed back enough to push his hands between us. His strong fingers pushing up between my thighs, sliding fully into my pussy. I bucked against him, the weight of his body only partially keeping me down onto the bed. The poor bed just groaning and creaking under us, as if not to be outdone by the sounds of pleasure escaping from me. I fell over the edge, again. The climax hitting me harder this time. Mikhail watched my face intently as I shivered though the orgasm. He looked fascinated by the way my body convulsed and trembled beneath him.

As he pulled his fingers from me, I could feel his cock against the inside of my thigh. His eyes locking with mine, I pulled him back down to my mouth. Kissing him and shifting my body so that I could feel the tip of him against my entrance. I wanted to hear more of those sounds he made in the shower. Wanted to feel him shiver like he had made me.

It didn't take any coaxing to have him shift his hips forward and drive into me as hard as he could. Mikhail pushed back, not enough to pull out, but so that he could look down, and see himself. I stretched my arms up to grip at his shoulders. Nails digging into this skin, which I may have broken with my nails. His movements were rough and quickly became erratic. The sounds from him were intoxicating. It was hard to control my grip on him, and I could feel just a faint bit of blood on my fingers.

I lost track of myself when my climax hit. My vision was filled with stars, and the vision of his panting lips. Mikhail wasn't far behind. His body stiffened against mine, coming almost to a stop. I squeezed him tighter with my shadows, pulling him against me until he let out a ragged exhale.

It took Mikhail a while to roll over to the side. Both of us were breathing heavily. The shadows receding back to my skin. It was a long time before I could form words to speak to him.

"I'm glad you decided this was a risk you were willing to take." I spoke softly through the ragged breaths. I felt him snake an arm under my shoulders, pulling me over so I could rest my body into his chest. Gazing down at his form, running my fingers across the top of his leg scars.

I really needed this. More than I thought.

The probably broken bed...maybe not so much.

Chapter 22

Mikhail

Over the next few weeks, the town was flooded with not only tourists but Federal Agents, county officials, and state white collars who got paid too much and spent way too much time shaking hands and talking to do anything to help. The Sheriff was more or less confined to his office, fielding phone calls and trying to save face in front of his superiors. He was definitely not getting re-elected.

Rose was so happy to help in the cleanup efforts at the mines that she sent coffee and food every chance she could send it up to the site. You would think some of the crew helping pull bodies from the mine in the mountain had never drunk anything but gas station coffee with the way they devoured the carafes she sent up. That's not even mentioning the donuts.

The Unknowns Department from my unit came to help with Liandra. Which meant I had to introduce them to Tailen. Which went about as good as I could expect. The two agents were wholly unprepared for the magnificence that she was when she wasn't hiding behind her spells. Though honestly, they were scared when Liandra appeared in front of them for the first time. I don't think I have ever laughed as hard when one of them had to go get himself a change of pants when she manifested for the first time.

With some pouring over her books and notes Tailen had figured out that she could confine Liandra's spirit to an object that she had in life. We had to figure out what would work though, and to do that we needed to be able to speak to her. After much discussion over Roses sandwiches and failed attempts, they decided to try a digital recorder. Not just any recorder though. They had to call in a favor and got one from a university that did research in Antarctica. It seemed to be able to withstand the chill when Liandra got near it. She had blatantly refused to possess another body, so it seemed like our only option.

Tailen was skeptical it would work, but luckily it did. She was able to tell us about a necklace that she had in life, a prized possession, that would have been in her childhood home. It took some time to track down, but Marcella found out that one of the tour guide's offices had a weird little museum of artifacts from the town's history. To be honest I think she was angrier that the antiques were not prop-erly archived and protected. She really deserved a museum rather than a small-town library, as impressive as it was. The owner agreed to give it up after Rose paid her a visit. Needless to say, that woman happily gave us whatever we wanted.

There was a town meeting at the city hall about halfway through the cleanup in which Marcella convinced the mayor that the mine needed to be turned into a memorial. That the town needed to step away from trying to hide its past, and that it needed to acknowledge it. It was decided that new paths would be put in to allow hiking up to the mine sites, after they had been cleaned up, and protections in place. Turn the site into a park, and have a memorial put up to honor those who died, and with Marcella leading the investigation they would find the names of each person who died in the tragedy of the mine collapse, along with those who died under the thumb of the corrupt business men that used to run this town.

Liandra agreed to the ritual that would bind her to the necklace. Tailen's promise to find a way for her to get a second chance at life. She was in her twenties when she died and spent the last few decades protecting the dead in a hole in the ground. She wanted to see the world. Liandra wasn't ready to move on, and Tailen was probably the only person who could actually figure out how to make that happen for her. There was a long discussion about making amends to the families of the men she killed; they were just as innocent as those she sought to protect. So, they made an agreement on that as well. Tailen said she would talk to Sal herself on behalf of Liandra and see if he even wanted to hear from her. In the end I don't think Sal was ready.

Tailen hadn't reactivated her sigil to cover her natural appearance since the night we returned to the motel. Not that she went flaunting around town, but she seemed to like not to care to hide. I'm pretty sure it was simply to get under the Sheriffs skin who could do nothing about her walking free. I enjoyed it as well, watching her with her long black hair down, her legs in those short shorts she always wore.

We spent time together when we could, and with Sal and Marcella, and Rose outside of the cafe. Tailen let me go hunting with her and Sal one night, which was very eye opening. I now knew why she didn't own any firearms, and why Sal was so hairy. They did however let me get a rather nice buck, and Tailen helped with tanning the skin. It had been a long time since I had been in the woods like that, and it felt amazing. Plus being able to share her company every night was more than I could have hoped for out of all this.

As the cleanup started to wrap up, the Feds started to leave, and the tourists started to lose interest. The town slowed back down.

It was a late night after being so at the mines all day. Tailen met me at her cabin, she was seated in the yard, a fire going in a makeshift pit. She didn't have shoes on and was staring intently into the flames, looking up only as I approached her and flopped onto the ground next to her.

"Did they get the shaft closed up? I know Liandra will be happy about that." She shifted closer to me, leaning on my shoulder.

"They did. The Unknowns guys are grateful for your help setting up sigils. I think they were too scared to actually tell you that though." I chuckled and put my arm around her.

Her body weight leaned into me, and she shifted closer. Her legs swung over mine and I could get a better look at her face in the flickering fire light.

"They really should get out of that basement and actually talk to some of the people they claim to be experts on."

"I can agree with that. Believe me, it's eye opening. I'm almost mad at myself for ignoring it. I also now know why Rose makes such good coffee. Never thought I would be drinking caffeine infused with succubus....aura? Is that the right word?" Tailen laughed loudly.

"I'm sure she will send you home with as much as you can put in the back of your SUV. I'm sure her pastries freeze well too."

"Yeah..." Going back to Detroit wasn't something I really had thought about at any length. Being here for just over two months it was a strange thought to go back to my sparse apartment, my desk in the office that would be covered in paperwork, the horrible lights of the break room and even worse office coffee.

I looked down at the woman who was laying on my chest. What I wanted was to not make the drive back alone. Somehow, I knew that wasn't going to happen. Tailen didn't seem like the person to just let what happened here go.

"Tailen, I don't want to ask. I really don't, but what do you plan on doing now?" I tightened my grip behind her back, because her answer was not something I wanted to hear.

"I have to go back there Mikhail. I missed something, someone. I have to know who did this. It's not just going to stop here. Like our Not-Charlotte said to me, they have time. I can't let Germany happen again." She looked up at me, her black eyes showed determination. Her voice though, was unsure. Was she conflicted? Her normal confidence was not present in her eyes.

"You could come with me. The FBI could give you resources, help track down anything you could need. I would be able to help you, the Unknowns department could...do nothing."

"I will appreciate anything you can do, but I can't come with you. I'm not part of your system, and I have a feeling that your department will feel conflicted about helping me enter into a country with their blessing, and me not being able to tell them what I am doing."

"We could at least get you paperwork, so you have travel documents, make it so you have backup if you need it."

"I have been traveling this planet for a long time Mikhail, I have very little need for documents."

"How will you get to Europe…do I want to know?" She chuckled a bit. I sometimes forgot she wasn't bound by the constraints that the rest of us were.

"How do you think I got here? I was locked up in a British museum storage warehouse before I got here. I know a woman who owns a boat that does transatlantic cargo. She will give me passage; I just work for the trip. I wouldn't mention that in your report though."

"Is it safe?" I shook my head. "That is a dumb question isn't it."

"No dumb questions. Yes, it's safe. She is someone to be trusted. I'm not going to tell her who she is though, so please don't ask."

"I will leave it alone. How long do you think you will be gone?"

That's when I felt her head bury back into my chest.

"I don't know. Months at least, but I can't promise a time-line. Especially if I also follow through with my promise to help Liandra.

"Would it be too much of me to at least ask that you keep in touch." I pushed her hair back around her ear and ran my fingers around to the back of her head.

"I would be glad to. As much as I can."

She leaned up and planted her lips on mine. It was long and soft. I felt her hands on the sides of my face. I savored the taste of her, this was the kiss that I didn't want to have with her. It meant that I wouldn't be seeing her for a long time.

"Can I ask you something?"

"Sure."

"Is Bigfoot real?"

"No....No he is not."

Acknowledgements

This book has been in the works for a long time now. I'm grateful that it's something that I have been able to pursue and spend free time on. I want to give thanks to those who have made this possible.

Zachary has been a constant source of encouragement for me. Letting me bounce ideas off him, to doing a first edit, and helping me figure out the back end of creating a book for publishing.

Stephanie you are nothing short of amazing. Editing my book from start to finish. Even though I know that it is not a genre you would normally consume. It means a great deal to me.

Scotty I will always be grateful that you were one of the first people to read through my book and give me some unhinged feedback.

To the rest of my Beta readers, friends, and family who let me talk about this project for the last couple years without judgement. Thanks.

I find it hard to express emotions in a way that accurately expresses my feelings and thankfulness for those who have made the process easy, and less scary. I have good people in my life, and I hope that with this weird little manuscript I have made them proud, and not regret helping me along the way. I do hope that all of you enjoy reading it as much as I enjoyed writing it.

About the author

Aleksandra Otto is an author from the weird and wonderful state of Ohio.

When she isn't delving into the word of the supernatural, she is usually drinking beer, hanging out at Renaissance Festivals, or crafting. She has been writing since she was young, and has an obsession with early 2000's crime dramas. She also enjoys reading horror graphic novels, romance books, and watching cartoons.

Sometimes her cat lets her write without yelling at her.